Hello!

Welcome to the third book in my Lost & Found series, all about Sasha, the band's lead singer! Sasha's story is a very personal one for me, but also one that I think will resonate with many of my teen and pre-teen readers. Have you ever felt out of your depth, worried that you weren't good enough? Ever wanted to hide away from reality or had a secret you were too scared to tell? If so, you'll understand Sasha's dilemma and love her journey to face the truth, find her courage and take back control of her life! Nobody's perfect, after all, and there's a real freedom in accepting that and choosing to be perfectly imperfect.

This is a book for anyone who has ever felt anxious or alone, anyone who's worried that their friends and family just won't understand. It's about facing up to what you want in life and letting go of what you don't . . . and it also follows your favourite Lost & Found characters as their career steps up a notch and they get the chance to record their first single!

Make yourself a fruit smoothie, curl up for a while and escape into a world of music, friendship, dreams and first love . . . with a few surprises in store along the way! Enjoy!

 xxx

Books by Cathy Cassidy

Lost & Found

LOVE FROM LEXIE
SAMI'S SILVER LINING
SASHA'S SECRET

The Chocolate Box Girls

CHERRY CRUSH
MARSHMALLOW SKYE
SUMMER'S DREAM
COCO CARAMEL
SWEET HONEY
FORTUNE COOKIE

LIFE IS SWEET

BITTERSWEET: SHAY'S STORY
CHOCOLATES AND FLOWERS: ALFIE'S STORY
HOPES AND DREAMS: JODIE'S STORY
MOON AND STARS: FINCH'S STORY
SNOWFLAKES AND WISHES: LAWRIE'S STORY

THE CHOCOLATE BOX SECRETS

ANGEL CAKE
BROKEN HEART CLUB
DIZZY
DRIFTWOOD
INDIGO BLUE
GINGERSNAPS
LOOKING-GLASS GIRL
LUCKY STAR
SCARLETT
SUNDAE GIRL

LETTERS TO CATHY

For younger readers

SHINE ON, DAIZY STAR
DAIZY STAR AND THE PINK GUITAR
STRIKE A POSE, DAIZY STAR
DAIZY STAR, OOH LA LA!

Cathy Cassidy

SASHA'S SECRET

PUFFIN

PUFFIN BOOKS

UK | USA | Canada | Ireland | Australia
India | New Zealand | South Africa

Puffin Books is part of the Penguin Random House group of companies
whose addresses can be found at global.penguinrandomhouse.com.

www.penguin.co.uk
www.puffin.co.uk
www.ladybird.co.uk

First published 2019

001

Set in 13.25/19.25 pt Baskerville MT Std
Typeset by Jouve (UK), Milton Keynes
Printed and bound in Great Britain by Clays Ltd, Elcograf S.p.A.

A CIP catalogue record for this book is available from the British Library

HARDBACK
ISBN: 978–0–241–38137–3

INTERNATIONAL PAPERBACK
ISBN: 978–0–241–38139–7

All correspondence to:
Puffin Books
Penguin Random House Children's
80 Strand, London WC2R 0RL

Thanks . . .

As always, thanks to my fab family, especially Liam, Cal and Cait.
Thanks to Helen, Mel, Sheena, Lal, Jessie, Fiona and all my lovely
friends for the hugs, pep talks and heart-to-hearts. Thanks to
Carmen, Amanda, Tania, Roz, Ellen, Lucie, Mary-Jane, Wendy,
Andrea and all at Puffin HQ; to Darley and his team for the
business bits; Martyn for the adding up; and Annie for arranging
my tour events. An extra big hug to Erin Keen for the beautiful
cover and artwork.

   This book was inspired by my daughter Caitlin, but additional
chats with readers Charlotte and Hollie and their mums also helped
hugely – many thanks. Cheers to Jen for the info on vocal coaching,
to Nicole for info on special effects make-up and to Cal for the info
on studio recording.

   Thanks to Tara Lyons, who bid in a charity auction to have her
name in the book – apologies for putting you up close and personal
with a hockey stick – and well done, Edinburgh Children's Hospital
Charity! Thanks to D & R, two fab readers whose names I
borrowed for this story, and of course to Mary Shelley the tortoise
for ongoing inspiration. The biggest thank-you of all goes to you, my
lovely readers . . . you really are the best.

Cathy Cassidy, xxx

1

Invisible Girl

When I was little, I loved to play hide-and-seek – even in our small terraced house I found hiding places everywhere. I hid in wardrobes, in cupboards, under the bed; I stood for hours behind the faded green curtains with just my feet sticking out, hardly daring to breathe.

My favourite hiding place was the cupboard under the stairs, behind the vacuum cleaner and the box of spray cleaners and the furniture polish that smelt like marzipan. I built a nest there, with a lumpy pillow and a blanket, making a chocolate-chip cookie last for an hour as I relaxed and let my mind drift.

I'd dream that I was up on stage singing, or dressed in tulle and pointe shoes, twirling my way through *Swan Lake*. I had a dozen different daydreams to suit my mood, and I could vanish into one whenever I wanted.

It was how I coped with the shouting.

Later Mum would cuddle me, tell me not to be scared. 'It doesn't mean anything,' she'd say, tucking me in at night. 'I haven't been feeling well and your dad's a bit stressed, but it'll pass. Just ignore it, pet!'

But I couldn't ignore it. Whenever things got bad, I could smell trouble in the air, feel the ground beneath my feet begin to slip. I'd ask Mum if we could play hide-and-seek.

'Oh, go on then,' she'd say, rolling her eyes, and I'd hear her counting slowly to a hundred as I ran to hide. I always felt safer burrowed away out of sight, lost in my dreams.

It didn't bother me that I might be waiting a couple of hours for Mum to remember I was hiding and come to find me. It didn't matter . . . I was safe.

It was just a bad patch, Mum said, the kind lots of couples have – but there were two years of uncertainty, of horrible rows and stony silences, of broken plates and dinners burned and cold and tipped into the bin. I found out much

later that Mum had been struggling after a miscarriage and that Dad had been trying to survive on a zero-hours contract. If Mum hadn't lost the baby, I'd have a little brother or sister now, but instead there was always something missing in our family, a ragged gap I couldn't even begin to fill.

Two years of hiding and wanting to vanish . . . and then everything changed.

I started school, Dad got a better job and Mum started working part-time in the beauty department of a big store in town.

'It'll be make or break,' she warned us, and for a while it looked like it might be the latter. Dad would come home tired and get annoyed because the house was untidy and there was no tea on the table. Mum would say she only had one pair of hands, that she was sorry if the house was a mess but life was never perfect.

I remember thinking that maybe she was wrong, that things could be perfect if you tried hard enough to make them that way. I remember thinking that Mum deserved that, and I wondered if it might be possible if I just tried hard enough. The next day I washed all the mugs and dishes in the sink, tidied my room and made Dad a cup of tea when he got in from work.

'You're a star, Sasha,' he said.

That was all I needed to start believing that perfection really was possible.

The rows began to ease up, and I convinced myself it was because I was trying so hard. The anger and resentment that had once crackled in the air between Mum and Dad faded away into silence, and they started smiling, laughing, hugging again.

I tried harder. I was helpful, cheerful, reliable. I brought home good school reports, never argued, got into the habit of setting the table, folding the washing, helping with the cooking.

'You're growing up,' Mum said. 'It doesn't seem so very long ago that I couldn't open a wardrobe without finding you sitting cross-legged among the coats and dresses, when you used to hide behind curtains with your feet sticking out at the bottom and think nobody could see you . . .'

I didn't tell her that wearing a good-girl mask was the best way of all to stay invisible.

I started secondary school, made friends, kept the mask in place. I wasn't super smart and I wasn't hopeless either,

just somewhere in the middle, but I always tried my best at everything. The teachers liked me, but not all the kids did.

The school bully, Sharleen Scott, labelled me 'Little Miss Perfect'. She was almost right, in an ironic kind of way, and also very, very wrong.

Underneath the try-hard exterior, I was a long way from perfect. Playing with my mum's make-up kit and singing into my hairbrush in front of the mirror were my only real skills. I had a morning make-up ritual using the samples Mum brought home from work. It was calming to brush on foundation and highlighter, as if I was painting on a second skin. I liked looking in the mirror and seeing a braver, brighter version of myself smile back.

I was an average student with a reasonable voice, a big imagination and a desperate need to please, but that's not what other people saw. They saw a girl who looked like she could take on the world, when actually I was hiding away from it. Ironic, huh?

Then a boy named Marley Hayes nagged me into auditioning for a band called the Lost & Found, and I ended up being their lead singer, which is kind of crazy. We've had some success, played a big festival, even been on TV.

I guess you could say it was all a dream come true. The trouble is, dreams aren't always the way you think they'll be. I like to sing, but I don't like being in the spotlight and I hate knowing that the band's success – or lack of it – hinges on me. What started off as performance nerves has evolved into the kind of anxiety that eats away at my confidence and keeps me awake at night. So yeah . . . now you know what's going on beneath the surface, and why I'm really not Little Miss Perfect. At all.

I may be the lead singer of the Lost & Found, but lately that feels more of a nightmare than a dream. I'm just bluffing my way through, hoping nobody spots that it's all smoke and mirrors.

I learned a long time ago that you can hide all kinds of stuff beneath a smile, an impression of careless confidence. Hopes, dreams, anxieties, fears . . . all those things stay safely hidden away when you know how to wear a bright, shiny mask over the top. I've had years of practice at hiding.

I am fourteen years old now and I have a theory.

I think that if you hide yourself well enough, and stay hidden, eventually you start to disappear for real . . .

SashaSometimes

273 likes

SashaSometimes So the Lost & Found made it to the TV news last night . . . how cool?
#Lost&Found #TVNews #CharityGig #TeenBand

littlejen You were so good! Tell Marley I love him!

MillfordGirl1 My favourite band!

JBSings I'd love to be like you, Sasha. Do you get nervous on stage?

SashaSometimes Oh my gosh, all the time! It's natural, though. That adrenaline can fuel a whole performance!

JBSings #MyHero

2

The Price of Fame

'Can I have your autograph?' the Year Seven boy at the bus stop asks. 'Saw you on TV last night – can you sign this?'

I smile and scribble my name on his homework jotter.

'You're my favourite,' he blurts. 'Out of anyone in the Lost & Found. I'm your number-one fan!'

He whips out a smartphone and snaps a quick selfie with me, then blushes a deep shade of crimson and lopes back to his mates.

I shake my head and smile, because I remember how it feels to be eleven years old and crushing on someone. In my case it was Harry Styles from One Direction, and if he'd ever signed the cover of my homework jotter I think I'd have fainted clean away with the shock.

The Lost & Found are not in that league yet, but still, I don't think I will ever get used to signing autographs. It's only really our lead guitarist Marley Hayes who gets a kick from it; he's crazy ambitious. Although the Lost & Found is a team, Marley is the driving force behind it. When I'm listening to his pep talks I almost believe that we can make the big time. Almost.

The bus appears at last and I head upstairs, where Romy's saved me a seat. She's my best friend, and she also plays violin and sings backing vocals with the band.

'See our bit on the local TV news last night?' she asks as I flop down beside her. 'Everyone's talking about it!'

'I just signed an autograph and had my photo taken by a fan,' I tell her. 'The price of fame!'

'Rather you than me,' Romy says. 'I'm glad I'm more of a background kind of person. Although even if I was lead singer, nobody'd want my picture!'

I nudge her sharply. 'Don't run yourself down, Romy! You're great! You just need to believe in yourself!'

Like me, Romy likes to keep things hidden, but she hasn't quite perfected the art of acting carelessly confident the way I have. Her anxiety shows, and that marks her out as vulnerable in a place like Millford Park Academy.

Romy pulls a face, laughing. A bunch of Year Seven girls shout over that we were brilliant on TV last night, and a Year Eleven boy called Matt Brennan wanders down from the back of the bus, dropping into the seat in front of us.

'Hey,' he says, pushing back an artfully tousled quiff and treating me to the kind of smile rarely seen outside a toothpaste advert. 'My name's Matt. I help edit *Scribbler* – you know, the school magazine. You're Sasha Kaminski, right? You're in that band, the Lost & Found, aren't you?'

'I'm the lead singer,' I say. 'Romy here plays violin and sings backing vocals . . .'

His eyes slide to Romy and then back to me again. 'Cool,' he says, and I find myself dazzled by his hazel eyes as well as the toothpaste-ad smile. 'So, yeah . . . I follow your Instagram, actually. It's cool. I wondered if I could interview you for the school mag? Get a scoop on what you're doing before you hit the big time?'

'Oh – we'd love that, wouldn't we, Romy?' I say.

'I was thinking more just you,' Matt says. 'And Marley Hayes, maybe. I know there are lots of you in the band, but I wanna focus on you and Marley, to begin with at least.'

I blink. I want to tell him about Lexie, who started the band in the first place. I want to tell him about Sami, whose artwork caused such a stir at the gallery the night before last, and how his awesome story would make a better magazine feature than anything me and Marley might have to say. I want to say that we're all equals, that Lee, George, Romy, Happi, Bex, Dylan and even Jake are just as important as anyone else, but in the end I don't. I allow myself to be dazzled by the smile, the eyes, the quiff.

'That'd be cool,' I say, and Matt grins and taps my mobile number into his phone before wandering back to his mates. It's Romy's turn to dig me in the ribs now.

'He likes you!' she whispers. 'I could tell! And you like him!'

'Nah, he's way out of my league,' I say.

'I don't see why,' she says. 'He might think he's Mr Popular, but actually he's just a boy with a hipster quiff and plenty of confidence. You're out of *his* league, I reckon! Besides, a girl can dream, right?'

I laugh, because I know Romy's right . . . Matt Brennan will be sneaking into quite a few of my daydreams from now on.

The bus pulls to a halt outside Millford Park Academy and Romy and I file down the stairs. Someone pulls at the sleeve of my blazer, and I turn to see school bully Sharleen Scott.

'Saw you on telly last night,' she says, so close I can smell the mixture of spearmint chewing gum and stale nicotine on her breath. 'Think you're quite something, don't you, Little Miss Perfect? Thing is, I see through the act. You're way out of your depth, Sasha. Why not just admit it?'

This feels too close to home, and for a moment I can't think of a smart reply . . . or any reply at all.

'Ignore her,' Romy says, trying to steer me away. 'She's just jealous!'

'Of you two? Don't make me laugh!' Sharleen snarls, turning her attention to Romy now. 'It's a shame TV makes everyone look bigger than they really are . . . a bit embarrassing, really. I don't know how you can stand up there, Romy, when you know everyone's laughing at you!'

My whole body flushes with anger, more on Romy's behalf than my own. I should feel sorry for Sharleen – I

know her spite stems from envy, from wanting to be part of the Lost & Found, but it's hard to be sympathetic. She gets a kick from hurting people, and she knows Romy is insecure about her looks.

I shake her hand off my arm and turn to face her, prickling with indignation.

'Just listen, Sharleen . . .'

And that's when it happens. I disappear.

Black hole, secret hiding place, silence.

I only know I've done it afterwards, when Sharleen is laughing and waving her hands about in front of my face, and Romy is asking if I'm OK.

I blink, pull in a deep breath and try to work out what I've missed.

'You're mad, you,' Sharleen says. ' "*Just listen*" . . . listen to what? The sound of freakin' silence?'

Romy hooks an arm through mine and drags me away, but I can still hear Sharleen jeering behind me.

'There's something wrong with you, you weirdo!' she crows, and although I tilt my chin up and pretend not to care, deep down I know she's right.

Hey Sasha, Matt here. Good to talk to you earlier and cool that you're happy to do something for the school mag. I was thinking we could give it the centre spread with lots of colour photos and use one for the cover too! #excited

Hi Matt – sounds great! We've got band practice after school – I'll tell the others & we can make a plan! Sasha x

OK! Could do something this weekend maybe? Get it sorted before half-term? I'd really like to see how the whole thing works, talk to you and Marley about how you see things going, that kind of stuff.

I'll ask Marley if you can come and watch our practice on Saturday. You can take some pictures and then do the interview bits? Sasha x

Perfect. Thanks for this, Sasha. Let me know what Marley says!

3

Black Holes

Some days are fine . . . just normal days, easy days, with no vanishing acts involved; other days are pitted with endless black holes for me to fall into. I can never tell exactly what each one will be like, although if I'm honest the good days are rarer now. There haven't been any totally clear days for a while.

The worst time of all was at the end of the summer holidays, when the Lost & Found played a live radio slot as part of a competition, showcasing a brand-new song. We were all crammed into a tiny studio, hot and bothered and determined to do our best and win the competition . . . and I zoned out. I missed my cue and by the time I realized that's what I'd done, the band had crashed to a halt in a mess of discordant chaos. We started again and I was OK, but we didn't win the competition and my confidence took a real dent that day.

'Don't worry about it,' Romy had said to me at the time. 'You're just a daydreamer – we all have our moments.'

Not everyone was so kind, though, and I know that unless I get my act together my days with the band are numbered. I haven't let them down that badly since, but the fear of it is always there, because I never know when a black hole will open up and suck me in.

And being thrown out of the band? I don't honestly know if that would be a disaster or a relief. What with the stage fright and the recurring black-hole moments, my head is one big mess of confusion lately.

Today, the black holes come thick and fast.

I lose the plot in games and fail to block a goal in netball, which earns me a telling-off from Ms Trent; I flunk a vocabulary test in French because I don't hear half the questions; I even zone out in the middle of eating and end up wearing a forkful of veggie lasagne on my Millford Park Academy jumper. Oops.

Lexie, Happi, Bex and Romy peer at me curiously as I scrub away the mess with a paper napkin, take off my jumper and stuff it into my bag.

'Everything OK?' Lexie asks. 'You seem distracted.'

'Probably dreaming about Matt Brennan,' Romy says. 'He was chatting her up on the school bus this morning. Reckons he wants to interview the Lost & Found for the school magazine.'

Bex raises an eyebrow. 'Matt Brennan, huh?' she says. 'Mr Heart-Throb himself!'

'He's not interested in me,' I protest, my cheeks pink. 'Just the band.'

'Maybe,' Happi says with a shrug. 'Good publicity to be in the *Scribbler*. Although Marley probably won't be impressed by anything less than the national newspapers!'

'Too ambitious for his own good,' Bex agrees. 'I just saw him outside the music room, signing autographs and smirking like the cat that got the cream. Says he's got some exciting news for us at practice later . . .'

'Hope he's not going to make us rehearse every day over half-term,' Romy groans. 'He's a slave driver!'

'He just wants us to get to the top, that's all,' Lexie says as the bell peals for afternoon lessons. 'But yeah . . . sometimes he is.'

Mum is working till six today, and Dad has a big building job to oversee, so once school is finished I hole up in Bridge Street Library, ploughing through my homework. It's cool and quiet and feels somehow safe, and I actually get some work done while sipping the orange squash Ms Walker, the pink-haired librarian, has made for me.

The Lost & Found get special treatment at the library because we helped to save it from closing; we campaigned like mad and played our first proper gig at a festival to save the libraries, and I don't think Ms Walker will ever forget it.

'Want a snack?' she asks. 'The Knit & Natter group left half a packet of chocolate digestives, and you haven't been home for your tea . . .'

'I'm fine,' I say, although the truth is I've had nothing since lunchtime and I won't be home until eight. 'Tonight's our treat night – Netflix and a takeaway. Don't want to spoil my appetite!'

'Lovely,' Ms Walker says. 'Enjoy it! I saw the Lost & Found on the news last night . . . the art gallery gig. I'm so proud of you all!'

I go back to my homework just as the first of several texts from Matt Brennan buzz through on to my mobile. The day hasn't been a total disaster – I got to talk to a very cool Year Eleven boy with a rakish quiff and hazel eyes, a boy who is texting me to arrange a weekend meet-up. OK, so the meet-up is a photo shoot and interview and not a date, but so what? It's a start.

I text back, smiling, knowing that a boy like Matt can't really be interested in me but liking the fantasy of it anyway.

I must have zoned out again somewhere along the line, because the next time I look up it's ten to five. I scoop my books into my bag and wave goodbye to Ms Walker before setting off across the park at a sprint. By the time I get to Greystones, the old mansion where our practice space is, my mobile says it's past five, and I hurry across the grounds towards the vintage railway carriage where the Lost & Found rehearse.

Marley is pretty strict about timekeeping, but it looks as though he's in a good mood today. It's unusually warm for autumn, and the whole band are sitting on the grass in the last dregs of afternoon sun, messing about with instruments and eating home-made flapjacks.

'Want one?' Happi asks brightly, holding out the tin. 'They're good!'

I smile and take a flapjack, sinking down on the grass beside my friends. Bex is reading *To Kill a Mockingbird*, Sami's sketching Lexie as she makes a daisy chain and Romy is playing the faintest whisper of a melody on her violin. Jake, the only one of the Lost & Found who doesn't play an instrument – he's our tech guy – takes a cold can of Fanta from under the old railway carriage and hands it to me.

'Thanks, Jake,' I say.

Sometimes the old railway carriage is my favourite place in the whole world.

'Good of you to join us, Sasha,' Marley comments, putting his guitar down. 'We couldn't start without our lead singer, could we?'

'Something cropped up,' I say, trying to sound casual. 'Won't happen again, promise.'

But it might, of course.

How do you explain that your life is suddenly full of black holes? That several times a day a tear in the universe might swallow you whole and spit you out again? I am no expert on astrophysics, but I learned enough from GCSE science to know that black holes can turn you inside out and stretch you out like a strand of spaghetti. I know that they're mysterious and dangerous, and that they distort time.

What's been happening lately seems a bit full-on to fall into the daydreaming category.

'So,' Marley says. 'Now we're all here . . . well, I wanted to say well done. You guys were amazing the other night. I think it's safe to say we're back on form – good work!'

'It was fun,' Bex says. 'And we didn't have to worry about Bobbi-Jo messing up on keyboards . . .'

Bobbi-Jo joined the band briefly in the summer, but she was cringingly bad – we all know Marley only wanted her in the band because her dad worked for the local radio station. Bobbi-Jo's with a hip-hop band now, and I've been filling in on keyboards. I sometimes think I'd be happier sticking to that than singing – less pressure.

'That slot on the local news last night was good,' Marley goes on. 'We need to keep pushing on the publicity front!'

'I was talking to Matt Brennan today,' I tell him. 'He asked me to have a word with you.'

'Dark-haired kid in Year Eleven?' Marley says. 'Bit full of himself? What did he want?'

'He wants to do a big feature on the Lost & Found,' I explain. 'Take some shots of our practice on Saturday and interview us . . . He reckons he'd get us on the cover.'

Marley laughs. 'Of the school magazine?' he scoffs. 'Big deal!'

'We've got a growing fanbase at school,' Lexie points out. 'Why not build on it?'

Marley shrugs. 'Matt's supposed to be OK with a camera,' he admits. 'And any publicity is good publicity, right? Yeah, tell him to come on Saturday. Why not?'

'Louisa Winter's exhibition has sold a load of paintings already,' Lexie chips in. 'They've raised lots of money – and awareness – for the refugee charity. And like Bex says . . . it was fun!'

'Not just fun,' Marley says. 'We were awesome. And I'm not the only person who thought so – Ked Wilder was

22

really impressed, he told me so. I didn't want to say anything until I knew it was happening, but – well, this is a massive opportunity for us. Our big break, if you like –'

'What is?' Lee interrupts.

'Big break?' Bex echoes.

'What massive opportunity?' Dylan asks. 'What are you talking about, Marley?'

'Give me a chance and I'll tell you!' Marley is enjoying the fact that he finally has everyone's attention. 'If you'll all just shut up for a minute. I need everyone to clear their diaries for half-term. I know it's a big ask, but this is important . . .'

'What is?' half a dozen voices demand.

'The Lost & Found are going to Devon for the week,' Marley announces. 'We'll be in Ked Wilder's studio, cutting our first EP with a sixties pop legend mentoring us every step of the way!'

There's a shocked silence, then a cacophony of excited whoops and yells, but all I feel is the sudden curdle of fear in my stomach.

SashaSometimes

163 likes

SashaSometimes Exciting news . . . can't say anything yet, but watch this space!
#Lost&Found #BigNews #TopSecret #Shhhhh #TeenBand

littlejen Ooh! Something to do with the Lost & Found?

Yorkie_Joe Recording deal?

Kezsez07 We need a clue! Please!

MillfordGirl1 #NeedToKnow

4

Treat Night

In case you think that things are still grim at home, I can tell you that they're really not. My parents work hard, but they're kind to each other and most of the time we're OK. I do my best to keep it that way.

Dad's a foreman with a small building firm, working with a team he's known for years now. The days of job uncertainty and low wages are over; Dad puts in long hours and is brilliant at what he does.

Mum loves her job on the beauty counter at Barlow's department store, and she's good at it too. Women drift past her counter feeling tired and drab, and Mum smiles and chats and sits them down, offers them a free mini makeover and her own personal brand of pep talk. When they look in the mirror, they see a whole new person gazing back – someone brighter, braver, ready for anything. Mum gives them a couple of free samples and they walk away feeling ten feet tall, and come back again and again to buy palettes of colour, jars of sparkle and pots of cream that smell of vanilla and adventure.

'I don't sell make-up,' Mum likes to say. 'I sell dreams.'

Three nights a week Mum cooks, and we eat healthy salads, fish pies, veggie bakes and green smoothies that taste a whole lot better than they look. Three nights a week Dad cooks, and we eat oven chips and microwave dinners, and sometimes his signature sausage and mash with onion gravy. On the seventh night we order a takeaway and pick a movie from Netflix, and nobody has to cook at all.

Tonight is takeaway night and Dad has ordered Indian. I don't think Mum's impressed, because they seem to be having a whispered conversation that halts abruptly when I arrive.

'Everything OK?' I ask. Dad says it's nothing, and Mum just says that curry gives her heartburn. She starts making a sandwich with peanut butter and sliced gherkins instead, and Dad rolls his eyes.

'Curry gives you heartburn but that little lot doesn't?' he asks, pulling a face.

She picks the film, a cheesy ancient American teen romance in which everyone wears dodgy clothes and the heroine is almost certain to choose completely the wrong boy. Dad threatens us with something bloodthirsty next week, but it doesn't matter because we're snuggled on the sofa, Mum wolfing her sandwich, me and Dad eating onion bhajis from the box.

'Good day at school?' Mum asks absently, her eyes still on the screen.

I could mention the black-hole moments, how they're getting worse, how they're scaring me . . . but that would worry my parents, of course.

'We had a French test,' I say, not mentioning that I flunked it. 'And I went to the library after so I'm pretty much up to date with my homework.'

'Good girl,' Dad says. 'The lads on the site saw you on TV last night. You've got some new fans there!'

27

'The girls at Barlow's were talking about it too,' Mum adds. 'I was ever so proud!'

'I signed my first autograph today,' I tell them.

'First of many, I bet,' Dad crows. 'My famous daughter!'

I pull a face. 'No way,' I argue. 'Not yet . . . anyway, it's a team effort. We're all in it together!'

Mum looks sceptical. 'You're the lead singer,' she says. 'The face of the band. That's why they're asking for your autograph, Sasha – get used to it!'

'I don't think I could ever get used to that kind of thing,' I say honestly. 'It's weird. Why should people treat us differently just because we've been on TV? We're no different from before! On the bus this Year Eleven boy from the school magazine – Matt, his name is – asked if he could take our photos at the practice on Saturday. He might put our picture on the cover – just imagine!'

'Why not?' Mum says. 'You're talented kids, all of you. So . . . is he nice, this Matt?'

'Mum!' I bluster. 'He's just a boy. I don't even know him!'

But my pink cheeks give me away, and Mum is smiling as she watches the movie. I swear she has a radar for this kind of thing. She can pick up the faintest flicker of excitement in my voice, the slightest sign of interest.

'I don't think you realize how good the Lost & Found really is,' Dad says, biting into a samosa. 'You've really got something. You could go all the way to the top!'

I squirm a little. It's great that my parents are proud of me, of course, but I feel a bit of a fraud. The thing is, I'm an average kind of girl. I get average grades, and without the help of make-up, my face is girl-next-door, not especially pretty, not especially plain. My blonde hair is probably my best feature, and even that has had a lot of help from wash-in hair colour. Until recently, I've never been the kind of girl to stand out from the crowd, but blending in isn't really an option when you're singing your heart out centre stage.

I wish my parents could be proud of me for something else, like my ability to stack the dishwasher without complaining or the fact that I can change a plug and make cheese sauce and do a pretty good cartwheel – not all at the same time, obviously.

When Marley first dragged me along to audition for the Lost & Found, the last thing I expected was to end up as lead singer. It was just a bit of fun at first, but then it got serious. Marley told me I'd get more confident with every performance, but I think the opposite is happening. And now, with the black-hole thing, everything seems so uncertain, so scary.

My parents are proud of me for something that is bound to go wrong, and when it does, I won't just let my friends down, I'll disappoint them too. Great.

Mum pokes me with one fluffy slippered toe. 'My daughter the pop star!' she teases, and I laugh and strike a pose, and the anxiety recedes for a moment.

'In my dreams,' I say.

'Dream on,' Dad says. 'Why not? Ked Wilder really rates you and he's a total legend – he must know what he's talking about!'

The mention of Ked Wilder brings me back down to earth with a bump, and I put down a half-eaten samosa and fix my eyes on the TV screen. The main girl character is trying to make a prom dress out of something hideous her dad has bought her, but I can't seem to focus on the movie at all.

What would happen if I just didn't mention Ked Wilder's offer?

My parents would find out sometime, though, and then I'd never hear the last of it. They're both very big on grabbing opportunity with both hands, and this is an opportunity all right.

I take a deep breath.

'Actually . . . Ked Wilder wants to get us into the studio at half-term,' I say, trying to sound casual. 'Which is cool, but it means going down to stay at his place in Devon, and it's really short notice, so I'd understand if you said no . . .'

Mum almost chokes on a sandwich crust. 'Say no?' she shrieks. 'Say *no*? Why would we do that? This is amazing, Sash! I mean it really is a once-in-a-lifetime chance . . . I'd go myself if I could! How did you manage to keep that one quiet?'

I fix on a smile. 'I just wanted to make sure you were both in a good mood before I mentioned it, that's all,' I bluff. 'It's such short notice and I don't think everyone's going to be able to make it . . .'

'But *you* will,' Mum says firmly. 'You're the lead singer – they need you. Just wait till we tell your gran. She had a poster of Ked Wilder on her bedroom wall when she was a teenager! She's not going to believe this!'

I roll my eyes and pretend to be engrossed in the movie, but inside I'm wishing there was a black hole handy – I'd jump right in and never come back.

Hey Sasha, all ready for the photo shoot and interview today. Where do I head for, exactly? You said the practice space is near Greystones? Is that the big mansion house across the park? Matt

That's the one. We could aim for one o'clock – that'd give you time to talk to Marley before practice starts. If you don't know Greystones, I can meet you at the bandstand in the park at ten to one. Sasha x

Cool – that way I won't get lost! See you then! M

5

Say Cheese

It's ridiculous to get excited about meeting Matt by the bandstand, I know. It's ridiculous to try on five different outfits, to style my hair in a ponytail, a French pleat and a messy updo before deciding to leave it down. I spend ages getting just the right understated cat's eye with my eyeliner, endlessly trying to choose between summer sandals and Converse.

It's ridiculous to bargain with the universe too, to pray that I won't blank out while Matt's around. I bargain anyway.

All the effort is worth it, just for the way Matt's face lights up when he sees me.

'Hey!' he says. 'Sasha! Thanks for agreeing to this! I'm really looking forward to meeting Marley and the rest of the band. I think I can do something really cool with this. If I get some good shots, I might try to place a couple of features in the Birmingham music mags!'

'Brilliant!' I say.

'It'd be great for me too,' Matt says. 'It's what I want to do – well, photography more than journalism, but it's all linked. If the photos and interview are good, we all win, right?'

'Definitely!'

Matt looks even cooler out of uniform, lean and long-limbed in skinny jeans and a vintage T-shirt, his camera slung round his neck. We fall into step, heading across the park and along the quiet avenue that leads to Greystones as Matt chats away easily. He's so easy to talk to – it's like we've known each other for ages.

'So how come your practice space is at Greystones?' he asks. 'Not that I'm complaining. It'll be a great location for the photo shoot!'

'Wait till you see it,' I say. 'You'll love it! We used to practise in the community room at the library, but when the libraries were threatened with closure a few months back we had to look for somewhere new. Our tech guy, Jake, lives in one of the apartments at Greystones. He found us the new place.'

Matt raises an eyebrow. 'And that's how you got involved in the music festival in the summer? It was all about saving the libraries, wasn't it? I came down and took some photos – you were amazing!'

I know he means the band, not me, but I can't help the quick flush of pink that stains my cheeks.

'It was our first gig,' I tell him. 'Talk about in at the deep end. But we saved the libraries and we got to meet Ked Wilder, so . . . well, it was pretty awesome, yeah!'

'Makes a great story,' Matt agrees. 'You've done brilliantly for such a new band and I've got a feeling this is just the start!'

I push open the gate at Greystones, and Matt steps on to the driveway, gazing up at the big old mansion in awe.

'Wow,' he breathes. 'I've seen the place from the park, obviously, but never up close. A crazy old lady artist lives here, right?'

I frown.

'Louisa Winter's not crazy,' I tell him. 'She's kind and creative and she's been really good to us. She was a model in the sixties, knew all sorts of cool people – and now she's a famous painter, of course. You should write something about her for the school magazine!'

'Um – maybe.'

I shrug. 'Anyway, we don't practise in the house. I'll show you . . .'

I lead Matt across the grass and through the trees until we emerge opposite the old railway carriage. Marley is sprawled across the steps playing guitar, lost in the moment, and Matt halts beside me, wide-eyed.

'Like it?' I ask.

'Awesome,' he says. 'Wow. This is where you practise? I love it! I had no idea!'

Almost unconsciously, he raises his camera and frames the view, and that's when Marley looks up. He doesn't look pleased to see us.

'Ah,' he says, curling his lip slightly. 'Camera Boy. I forgot about you.'

Matt blinks. 'I arranged with Sasha to take some photos, do an interview –' he begins.

'For the school magazine, I know,' Marley interrupts, faking a yawn to underline how unimpressed he is.

'Marley!' I say. 'You agreed to this. You said it was fine! What's the problem?'

He puts down his guitar and stands up, stretching lazily as if this whole meeting is one big headache.

'Whatever,' he says, frowning at Matt. 'No problem. You're here now. May as well stick around. I'm Marley Hayes.'

Matt drags up his best smile. 'I know, I've seen you around at school – I'm Matt. I won't get in the way. I just wanted to ask a few questions, take some shots as you practise and then set up some more styled pictures. I can guarantee you the cover slot on the next issue, and the plan is to send out some stuff to the local music mags in Birmingham, see if they'll bite . . .'

'The local music press?' Marley questions. 'Why not the nationals?'

Matt grins. 'Sure!' he says. 'Why not? I like your stuff. I've been following you since you played the festival in the park and I think you have massive potential. I just want to help get that message out there. I'm serious about what I do and I can see you are too. It makes sense to work together, right?'

Marley shrugs. 'I'll talk to you,' he agrees. 'You can watch us practise, chat to the others, take as many pictures as you like. Once I've seen the results, I'll tell you whether we can work together.'

He turns and heads into the old railway carriage, and Matt and I exchange silent and slightly horrified looks.

'It'll be OK,' I promise, with no clue whether it will be or not.

In the end, it's more than OK. Matt takes out a notebook and we sit on the steps while he asks me some questions, which bugs Marley enough to make him come out and sit with us. Pretty soon he's telling Matt everything there is to know about the Lost & Found, along with his plans for world domination. By the time the others start to arrive, Matt has filled pages of his notebook and Marley's bad mood has started to lift.

Matt stays in the background while we practise, moving quietly around, the click of his camera lost beneath the music. Marley, hyper aware we're being observed, pushes everyone to the limit. The result is possibly the best practice we've ever had, and when I glance across at Matt as I belt out the finale of 'Setting Sun' I can see he's impressed.

'Sasha?'

I blink, stepping back from another black-hole moment to find everyone looking at me. Clearly my bargaining with the universe has not worked after all.

'Sorry . . . what?'

'You missed your cue,' Marley says. 'I wanted us to run through 'Song for the Sea' one more time, but you were miles away!'

'Daydreaming,' Jake says, offering me a ready-made excuse. 'You creative types are all the same. Want a chocolate lime?'

A wrapped sweet flies through the air and I catch it with shaking hands, try for a smile.

Marley rakes a hand through his hair. 'Let's call it a day,' he decides. 'Well done, people – that was good work. If you can all hang around a little while, Matt here is planning on taking some more photos – everybody out!'

'Well, not quite everyone,' Matt says sheepishly. 'I mean, we won't need you . . . Jake, is it? Mr Tech Guy? Just the people actually in the band!'

'Jake's in the band,' Bex says. 'Just because he's behind the scenes doesn't mean he's not one of us!'

Matt grins. 'I know – obviously!' he backtracks. 'And he's in some of the rehearsal shots, of course. But for the posed ones . . . just the musicians. OK?'

'OK with me,' Jake says with a shrug. 'I can help if you like? Photographer's assistant?'

'Don't need one,' Matt says bluntly.

I don't think Matt means to be quite so dismissive, but I feel a bit sorry for Jake as he slopes off home across the grass.

Any awkwardness is soon forgotten, though. Matt's in his element, arranging us all on the steps of the old railway carriage, then under the trees, then clowning about in an overgrown flower bed. He lines up the band in front of the railway carriage and gets Marley, Lexie and me to go inside and lean out of the carriage windows.

'Say cheese!' Matt yells, and a cheesy chorus erupts. We're having fun.

Later, Marley sits on the steps and flicks through the images on Matt's camera, his face impassive.

'Think we just got ourselves an official photographer,' he says at last, and Matt rolls his eyes and laughs.

To the parent/guardian of Sasha Kaminski,

You and Sasha are cordially invited to an informal meeting at Greystones House at 7 p.m. on 10 October to discuss the band's proposed trip to my Devon studios during October half-term. As you already know, the Lost & Found are a very talented group of young people. I hope to work with them to maximize their potential and hopefully help them to step up to the next level.

If your child is interested in taking part, please do come along to the meeting – it makes more sense to answer your questions in person than to try to explain by letter. Oh, and Louisa says there will be cake!

Best wishes,

Ked Wilder

6

Tea and Cake

'Seriously, Mum, it's a crazy idea,' I argue. 'It's a brilliant opportunity, but dragging the whole band down for a week in Devon at half-term? With hardly any notice? I don't think it'll happen, that's all!'

Mum sighs. 'I thought you'd be excited,' she says. 'I would be, in your shoes. I thought you'd be the one nagging me to let you go, not the other way round!'

'I *am* excited,' I say, although to be honest 'scared' is a far better word to describe how I'm feeling. I should be thrilled at the idea of working with Ked Wilder . . . but that was before little chunks of my life started disappearing, a bit at a time, always at the most awkward moment possible.

How can I 'step up to the next level' as lead singer of the Lost & Found when I can't even navigate my school day without looking like an idiot?

It's just a matter of time before the band start looking at me with the same disappointment as my teachers. And it'll happen way faster if we're all stuck in a studio together, practising 24/7 with pop legend Ked Wilder watching our every move. I've been in denial, but tonight's meeting at Greystones is threatening to make it all too real. I don't want to go – not to the meeting, not to Devon.

'It'd be amazing,' I tell Mum now. 'If it happened. But Romy won't be able to leave her mum – she's ill a lot and totally relies on her. And Happi's parents are super strict – I can't see them agreeing to send her to Devon for a week. I don't think Sami, Bex or Lexie are sure about it either, and there's no point unless the whole band are there.'

Mum frowns. 'It's not like you to be so negative, Sash,' she says. 'Is everything OK?'

This is my chance, my opportunity to tell Mum what's been happening . . . but how can I when I don't understand it myself? I know it's happened in front of my parents a few times: 'Dreaming again, Sasha!' they say, or, 'Hey,

45

are you listening?' It probably doesn't seem anything to worry about, just me being ditzy and dreamy again. How do you tell your mum you keep falling into a black hole and vanishing? It sounds like the plot of an especially bad sci-fi movie – she'd think I was crazy. Sometimes I think so too.

'Sash?'

'Everything's fine,' I mumble. 'I just hope this meeting isn't a waste of time, that's all . . .'

'It won't be.' Mum grins, grabs her best coat and chucks me my jacket. 'We'd better go, though, or we'll be late. Your dad's working till eight, so he won't make it.'

'Again?' I say. Dad seems to have been working every shift he can get lately, which makes me anxious. 'He works too hard!'

'He's just doing the best he can for us,' she declares. 'C'mon – whether the trip comes off or not, we still get to meet the famous Ked Wilder and eat cake . . . what's not to like?'

I'm laughing as she bundles me out of the door.

The meeting doesn't pan out quite the way I imagined.

Louisa Winter opens the door to us, looking even more dramatic than usual in a vintage emerald dress with a handkerchief hem, her auburn hair piled up on her head and secured with a couple of chopsticks.

'Ooh, I love your dress!' Mum gushes. 'I can tell you're a painter, Ms Winter – you have a wonderful eye for colour! I always notice these things. I'm a make-up artist, you see. I work in Barlow's department store in town. We have some fabulous jewel-bright eyeshadows, really intense and shimmery. You'd like them!'

'Perhaps I would,' Ms Winter says graciously. 'Maybe I'll pop along one of these days! Come in, both of you. There's tea and cake – and Ked's here, of course. We're almost ready to start.'

The big, shabby-chic sitting room is crammed with people. I see Romy and her mum, Happi and her parents, Bex and Lexie and their foster parents – even Lexie's grandparents. Lee's dad is there in oil-stained overalls, and Marley and Dylan's mum is sitting nervously on the edge of one of Louisa Winter's squashy sofas, still in her supermarket tabard, balancing a china cup and saucer anxiously on one knee. George's dad is wearing a tweed jacket and twiddling his moustache, and Sami's mum and sister are chatting to a woman in a billowy Indian dress who can only be Jake's mum.

Jake waves me over, but as I move towards him I'm distracted by a friendly nudge from someone I really didn't expect to see. Matt Brennan grins at me, notebook and pencil at the ready, his mum perched beside him on a slightly moth-eaten chaise longue.

'Sasha! I saved a space for you,' he says, as Mum and I pick our way through the sitting room in search of the last remaining chairs. 'Thought you weren't coming for a minute there!'

'Wouldn't have missed it for the world,' I tell him, and I almost mean it too, now that I get to sit next to Matt. He saved a seat for me . . . That has to mean he likes me, right?

I smile apologetically at Jake, but he's turned away already.

'The cake is to die for,' Matt whispers, as Louisa Winter approaches with a plate piled high with home-baked goodies. I choose what looks like a slice of lemon drizzle, while Matt snaffles a second piece of chocolate gateau.

'Lapsang, Earl Grey, orange pekoe or squash?' Louisa Winter asks, and I ask for squash because I have no clue what the other options might involve. We have PG Tips at home.

'I didn't know you'd be here,' I whisper to Matt. 'It's a nice surprise!'

'For me too,' he replies. 'We got the letter from Ked Wilder yesterday – how cool?'

'Very,' I agree. 'Brilliant, in fact! Why d'you think he asked you?'

'Well, it's not like it's just the band, is it? Jake's going, and all he does is twiddle with the mixing desk and set stuff up, right? Ked's probably got people to do all that already.'

I frown. 'Jake's great, and he's definitely part of the band. You'd like him, actually!'

'Yeah?' Matt says with a shrug. 'Anyway, seems Marley wanted me to come to Devon as official band photographer, and Ked loved the idea. So here I am!'

He winks and grins, and a flutter of butterflies start doing somersaults in my belly. Suddenly the trip to Devon seems a whole lot more appealing.

The buzz of chatter and the clink of mismatched china teacups stills abruptly as Ked Wilder strides into the room, all long legs and black leather jacket and fedora hat. Mum, sitting across the room with George and his dad, looks bright-eyed and pink-cheeked, and she's not the only one displaying middle-aged fangirl tendencies. I try not to cringe.

'Hello!' Ked Wilder booms. 'Thank you all for coming along this evening, and at such short notice too. I called this meeting because I really wanted to meet you, and I wanted to explain why I'd like the kids to come down to the studio at half-term. We all know how talented the Lost & Found are, but it's a long time since I've seen such drive and enthusiasm in a young band.

'I've been in this business a long time, and I believe these kids have something special – they could go all the way to the top. I want to help in any way I can, and if we can get everyone together down in Devon . . .'

'How long are we actually talking?' Lee's dad wants to know.

'Five or six days?' Ked suggests. 'We could get a lot of very useful stuff done in that time. School breaks up on the

Thursday – Friday's an Inset day it seems, so the kids can travel then. I'll send them back the following week. Before anyone asks, I'll be covering travel costs – a hired minibus seems the best plan – and I'll put everybody up at my home. It's a big house and I have a great team – we'll make sure everyone is looked after.'

There's a murmur of appreciation, but not everyone is convinced.

'Well,' Happi's mum says. 'It's very generous, and I don't want to seem ungrateful, but I'm not sure I'm comfortable with my daughter going away for a week with no real supervision . . .'

'I worry about this also,' Sami's mum says.

Ked Wilder nods. 'I'd be the first to admit that looking after a bunch of teenagers will be daunting,' he says. 'So I'd like to ask if any of you parents would like to come along to keep it all running smoothly. That way I can focus on what I'm good at – the music! We've room for three or four adult guests to accompany the band if anyone's up for it?'

The discussion shifts to include several parents who are offering to act as chaperones, and Ked Wilder gets out a notebook to jot down names and contact numbers.

'I can't,' Mum whispers sadly. 'I'd give anything to be able to go, but I've taken extra shifts all through half-term and your dad will still be in the middle of this new estate build. He can't take time out.'

Mum and Dad seem to be working all hours lately, and I remember the whispered conversation from the other night and how they put on hasty smiles the moment I came in. A flicker of disquiet grows inside me. Is something wrong?

'I don't mind staying home, cooking the tea and keeping you both company, if it helps?' I offer, but I know it's a losing battle.

'No way,' Mum says. 'You're going, Sash. You can't let an opportunity like this go by. It's your dream!'

If only she knew.

Is it OK to text so late? Just wanted to thank you for setting up the photo shoot. I'd never have approached Marley without your back-up – he's pretty spiky, isn't he? He liked the photos, though! Anyway, thanks to you, looks like I'll be coming down to Devon at half-term – can't quite believe it! Matt

S'OK, can't sleep. Thinking about the Devon trip. I mean, obviously, a dream come true, but also scary! Sasha x

Don't be scared! This could be your big break! If Ked Wilder propels you into superstardom, remember I'll be running along behind, taking loads of pictures! M

Stop it, you're making me laugh! Sasha x

Good! Seriously, I have no shame. I plan to hang on to your coat tails for the sake of my own career! M

You don't need us. You're amazing already! I'm glad you're coming on the Devon trip, though. That's cool. Sasha x

It'll be fun, Sasha. Promise. G'night! M

G'night! Sasha x

7

Sorry

The weather turns cold and wet overnight, but I'm in denial, heading to school without the nylon waterproof Mum tries to foist on me. I live to regret it. By the time I get to the bus stop my hair is drenched and plastered across my face in rat's tails, and my attempt to stay upbeat is drowned beneath the tidal wave that engulfs me as the school bus zooms past without stopping, ploughing through a puddle the size of a small lake.

On days like this the very last thing you need is games, but that's exactly what lies in store in period three. The rain has eased off, but I'm hoping Ms Trent will keep us inside anyway because it's blowing a gale out there and I'm still soggy from my soaking earlier.

No such luck.

'What you need is a good, brisk game of hockey to warm you all up,' she declares.

I groan, dragging on my PE kit, the ugliest T-shirt and shorts combo in the northern hemisphere, made from a slimy man-made navy fabric decorated with alarming stripes of neon tangerine. Put it this way, if I were to get lost in a thick fog miles from anywhere, I'd still be visible, even from outer space. I bet the space rescue team would need to wear shades to protect their eyes from the migraine-inducing tangerine stripes.

'Get going, girls!' Ms Trent barks. She hands out lethal weapons, otherwise known as hockey sticks, and we jog down the side of the football pitches. The boys are nowhere to be seen. Their teacher is a lot less savage than Ms Trent, so they're probably in a nice heated gym doing bench presses and sit-ups.

It's freezing, but the running does warm me up, and by the time we've done five circuits of the hockey pitch my heart is thumping and the breath is warm and ragged in my throat. Ms Trent divides us into teams, and I end up as a forward, actually scoring two goals and earning some praise from Ms Trent for a change.

I'm almost enjoying it, way more than Romy who's lurking at the far end of the pitch and looking like she might die of either boredom or exposure at any minute. The ball flies past me again, and I scoop it closer and start to leg it down the pitch in case I can make it three goals. I'm buzzing, grinning, on a mud-stained hockey high . . . and then I'm not.

I'm nothing.

The world slips away and I'm nowhere at all, lost so far from home that not even that imaginary rescue team in outer space could find me. And then I hear shouting somewhere on the edge of my consciousness, and shame curdles in my belly before I can gather my thoughts and work out that, yes, it's happened again.

'. . . never seen anything so idiotic! You're a good player when you want to be, but that was downright dangerous. Good grief! What were you thinking?'

'Miss, I don't think she's very well . . .'

'Not well? Rubbish! Are you even *listening* to me, Sasha?'

57

'Sasha? Sasha, can you hear me?'

Someone has an arm round my shoulder, and as my eyes focus I see Romy beside me, her face anxious, while Ms Trent glares, her expression icier than the October chill.

A girl called Tara Lyons from the other team is sitting on the grass at my feet in a tangle of hockey sticks, splattered with mud and with a thin trickle of blood coming from her nose. Guilt floods through me, although I have no idea what I've done. I just know that somehow this is my fault.

'What happened?' I whisper.

'She ran into you,' Romy tells me. 'You stopped and Tara tripped and managed to get up close and personal with your hockey stick. It was an accident . . . I don't think she expected you to stop so suddenly . . .'

How could she, when I had no idea myself?

I reach out a hand to help Tara up, but she says something very rude under her breath and scrambles to her feet without my assistance. Ms Trent hands her some tissues to staunch the nosebleed and tells me to take her to the medical room and then go to the changing rooms and wait.

'I'm not happy with your behaviour lately,' she tells me crossly. 'Not at all. Right. Enough time-wasting!'

She blows the whistle to restart the match a little too shrilly. I feel the screech is hollowing out my insides, stripping back my skin. I've gone from boiling hot to freezing cold in the space of thirty seconds, and I'm shaking all over. I can't tell whether it's the shock of being yelled at or something to do with the black-hole moment.

Tara is stalking away across the playing field. Her nose may be bleeding, but her legs are working fine, and I have to run to catch up.

'I'm sorry,' I say, struggling to keep up with her. 'I don't know what happened back there. One minute I was running after the ball, the next everyone was yelling and you were on the floor, all muddy and battered. If I hurt you . . . well, I'm gutted! I didn't mean to!'

Tara gives me a sidelong glance. 'I bumped into you, OK? I was running too, trying to get the ball, and then you stopped dead and I just sort of crashed into you. It had to be deliberate. Why else would you just freeze like that?'

'I don't know!' I say. 'Maybe it was some kind of blackout? I'm sorry!'

59

'Like that helps,' she says, as we skirt the outdoor lunch area and push through the double doors back into school. 'You're saying you don't remember anything? Seriously?'

'Seriously,' I promise. 'It's happened before, but nobody's been hurt. I'm so sorry!'

'Can you stop saying that? It's not helping.'

'Sorry!'

She glares at me over the top of the bloodstained tissues.

'OK,' I backtrack. 'I'm . . . um, I won't say it again.'

We arrive at the nurse's office and Tara lowers the wad of tissues to give me a weary look. Her nose is a peculiar shade of blotchy crimson, but the bleeding seems to have stopped.

'If you're having blackouts, you're the one who should be seeing the nurse,' she says.

'No, no, I can't do that,' I argue. 'It's nothing, really!'

Tara rolls her eyes and raises her hand to knock on the office door, but at that moment it opens and Jake appears, holding an ice pack to his temple.

'PE can be very dangerous,' he says, eyeing Tara. 'Right?'

She sweeps past him into the office and slams the door behind her.

'Something I said?' he asks, looking slightly hurt.

'Something I did, I think.' I sigh, and the words come pouring out before I have time to think. 'It's me she's mad at, not you. I . . . kind of zoned out in the middle of a hockey match, and she ran into me and got a faceful of hockey stick . . .'

I fade into silence. Jake has seen me zone out before, but, like the rest of the band, he seemed to think I was just a bit daydreamy and distracted. I've just given myself away big style, but he seems not to notice.

'Ouch,' he says. 'Ice-pack treatment for Tara too then, I think! Want a chocolate lime?'

He takes a crumpled packet from his pocket, grinning, and I accept, grateful for the small sugar rush.

'Thanks. What happened to you?'

'Fell off the vaulting horse,' he explains. 'I was seeing stars for a minute, which is why they sent me here, to be on the safe side. I'm OK, though. Just very accident-prone!'

He grins sheepishly, and for one moment I think I've got away with it. I am caked in mud and wearing neon nylon, sure, but my black-hole secret remains safe.

Or not.

'This zoning-out thing,' Jake says into the silence. 'It's happened before, hasn't it? In practice sometimes . . . and at the radio station that time, when we were in the Battle of the Bands?'

Shame floods through me and my cheeks are blazing.

'I have to go,' I mutter.

'Aren't you staying to see the nurse?' Jake asks. 'I thought –'

'You thought wrong. I don't need to see the nurse. I'm fine!'

Jake puts a hand out and tugs my sleeve, and I turn back.

'Can I ask you something?' he says awkwardly. 'Are you going out with Matt Brennan?'

My eyes widen. 'Of course not!' I snap. 'Not that it's any of your business, Jake!'

He shrugs and bites his lip. 'No, obviously,' he says. 'It's just . . . I've heard he's a bit of a user, that's all. A bit of a chancer. And I wouldn't want you to get hurt!'

I shake my head, furious. 'I won't get hurt,' I say. 'Because there's nothing going on between me and Matt – we're just friends. And if you were a friend, Jake, you wouldn't try to tell me what to do, or who I can and cannot see!'

I pull away and storm along the corridor, blinking back tears.

'Sasha, wait, that's not what I meant –'

'Gotta go,' I yell over my shoulder. 'Forget it, Jake. I'm OK!'

But I know that it's no use pretending any more, because I'm not OK . . . I'm not OK at all.

SashaSometimes

189 likes

SashaSometimes Daydreaming . . .
#RainyDay #SchoolDay #Lost&Found #Dreamer

PetraB First like!

littlejen Second like!

OllieK Are you thinking up new songs?

Brownie You're my dream girl!

MattBFotos Nice shot . . . cute!

8

Kidnapped

Once the tide of escaping pupils has ebbed to nothing and the last school bus has pulled away from the kerb, I leave the safety of the empty corridors and make for the gates. I'm just stepping on to the pavement when someone grabs my arm.

'Gotcha!' Jake says, as Lexie, Sami and Romy close in from the other side. 'We wondered where you were hiding!'

'Gettoff!' I say, glaring. 'What is this, some kind of ambush?'

'More of an apology,' Jake says under his breath. 'I'm an idiot sometimes . . .'

'We're kidnapping you,' Lexie tells me brightly. 'Taking you for a hot chocolate at the Leaping Llama!'

'We wanted to check you were OK,' Romy adds. 'You missed the bus and got soaked on the way to school, and Ms Trent went overboard in hockey. Then you went missing at lunchtime and you weren't at the bus stop either!'

She tucks an arm through mine, and this time I don't pull away.

The Leaping Llama is one of those painfully hipster cafes where the waiters have beards and man-buns, and roll up the cuffs of their skinny jeans to show off their sock-free ankles. It also happens to do the best hot chocolate in Millford, and today I reckon I've earned one.

'I've never been kidnapped before,' I say, attempting a wobbly smile.

'We're the best kidnappers ever,' Romy promises. 'Most hostages only get bread and water – you get hot chocolate!'

Jake steers me towards a corner booth while the others head to the counter to order.

'I'm sorry,' he says again. 'I heard some stuff and I didn't want you to get hurt, but I should have kept my mouth shut . . .'

'You should,' I growl.

66

'Look, don't hate me, Sasha. I was trying to do the right thing – I just misjudged it.'

'Matt Brennan's OK!' I argue.

'If you say so . . .'

'He is! You'd like him if you just gave him a chance!' I insist, but I remember how offhand Matt was with Jake at the photo shoot and know that's probably not true. I sigh. Matt may not be perfect, but it's too late now to tell me not to fall for him. I've fallen – hook, line and sinker.

'It's only because I care,' Jake says.

'I'm fine! Matt's just a friend and the zone-out thing is probably nothing. Don't say anything in front of the others – they'd think it was weird . . .'

He raises one eyebrow. 'We're your friends,' he says. 'If something's wrong, we want to help.'

'I'm OK!'

But suddenly I'm tired of pretending everything's OK. My shoulders slump and a single tear slides down my cheek. 'Look, I don't know what the zone-out thing is and I don't know why it happens,' I say in a whisper. 'That day in the radio station when we were recording live for Battle of the Bands . . . that was the first time I noticed it. You saw, right?'

Jake nods.

The whole band had been crammed into a hot and crowded radio studio to play live for a local competition. I remember being nervous as the first chords rang out, and the next thing I knew everyone was staring at me as the music crashed to a ragged, discordant halt. I'd totally missed my cue – on live radio. That was the day my confidence shattered into about a million pieces and, no matter how hard I try to put it together again, I can't seem to manage it.

'It's happening more and more,' I say. 'Every day. There's no warning, and I never know what's happened until I come back to myself and realize people are staring, or shouting or whatever. It's horrible!'

He frowns. 'You can't keep something like this to yourself,' he tells me. 'Tell your parents. Tell your friends. See a doctor. Get some help!'

'I will,' I say. 'But I'm still getting my head round it. Things are a bit weird at home just now – money problems maybe. And it's not the right time to tell the band. I don't want to drag everyone down, be the weak link. Marley would chuck me out!'

'No chance,' Jake says.

'I think he would,' I argue. 'After the Devon thing, I'll tell my parents. I can't say anything yet, though. It'd just mess things up for everybody!'

I can see Jake thinking this over, not convinced.

'What's it feel like?' he asks. 'When you zone out?'

I frown. 'Hard to explain. It's like I go somewhere else . . . slip into some parallel universe, or fall into a black hole or something. It's like the memory of what's happened is just out of reach, no matter how hard I try to hold on to it. I'm the invisible girl!'

'You're not invisible,' Jake says. 'I can see you. You're still here.'

He looks at me so intently for a moment that my heart starts to thump, but just then Lexie, Romy and Sami return, squeezing in beside us and chatting loudly. The awkwardness dissolves and, even though he hasn't promised to keep my secret, Jake doesn't mention the zone-outs again.

'Hot chocolate is on the way,' Lexie announces. 'Best remedy ever for a rubbish day!'

'Ms Trent was totally out of order this morning,' Romy is saying. 'It was just an accident – could have happened to any of us.'

I grin, grateful for the kindness.

'Tara's fine now,' she tells me. 'No harm done.'

My friends seem more interested in the imminent arrival of our hot chocolates, carried by an especially theatrical waiter in horn-rimmed glasses and a tweed waistcoat complete with pocket watch and chain.

'Five deluxe hot chocolates with whipped cream and dipping flakes,' he announces, setting the tray down between us. 'We're trialling a new range of raw gluten-free, sugar-free vegan cakes . . . cacao, kiwi and lime drizzle cupcakes with cashew cream. Try them with our compliments and tell us what you think!'

He strides back to the counter, leaving us slightly befuddled.

'Raw cakes?' Sami echoes. 'Really?'

'What actually are they?' Romy says with a frown. 'How d'you get cream from a cashew nut?'

'My mum makes raw vegan cakes sometimes,' Jake says. 'They taste better than they sound!'

And it turns out that the cupcakes are great, sweet and tangy, a perfect foil for the richness of the hot chocolate. For a moment we're all silent, spooning up cream and

cake and sipping the thick, warm chocolate, and I think that there's nowhere I would rather be than right here, right now, with these people who really care about me.

Talk turns to the trip to Devon, scheduled to set off on Friday. Ked Wilder has arranged a minibus to take us down, and three adults have signed up to go along and keep an eye on us: Jake's stepdad, Sheddie, and Lexie and Bex's foster carers, Mandy and Jon.

'Not sure what they're actually going to *do*,' Lexie says. 'It'll be a bit boring for them while we're recording. Still, the minute Ked Wilder asked for volunteers I knew they'd offer!'

'My stepdad'll just chill,' Jake says. 'Sheddie's OK . . . practical and pretty laid-back.'

'I don't know what they think we'll be getting up to,' Lexie adds. 'From what Ked Wilder was saying, we'll be so busy with the music we'll have no energy for anything else!'

'My family are keen for me to go,' Sami says. 'It is a good opportunity! And perhaps it will be fun?'

I know there hasn't been much fun in Sami's life these last few years, so I can see how this might appeal.

'Hope so,' Romy says. 'I honestly didn't think I'd be able to come, but Mum was determined. She's organized her

71

cousin to come down from Scotland and look after her while I'm gone.'

Nobody is more astonished than I am that Romy's coming on the trip to Devon. If she'd backed out, I'd have felt less guilty about doing the same, but everyone's so excited I feel I can't cry off. Besides, my parents would never forgive me.

Lexie takes a bite of her chocolate flake and grins. 'Six whole days working with Britain's best-loved pop legend. It's going to be so cool!'

'He probably lives in a mansion,' Romy says. 'I mean, he's pop royalty, isn't he? Imagine someone like that being interested in us!'

'Ked believes in us,' Sami says. 'He must know everyone in the music business. This could really change things for us!'

Jake spoons up the last of his hot chocolate, watching me, and somehow his blue-eyed gaze dislodges the cool-girl mask I'm trying to hold in place.

'I'm dreading it,' I blurt, and everyone stares at me, wide-eyed. 'I mean, there's so much riding on this! What if I mess up, let everyone down?'

The words are out now. It's like I've let the genie out of the bottle, and there's no way of getting it back in again.

'Is that all?' Jake says, breaking the silence. 'Trust me, Sasha, we're all a bit wary – even me, and I'm not properly part of the band! This is a big deal – for all of us, and for the Lost & Found as a whole. We'd be weird if we didn't have some worries!'

'I am terrified too,' Sami admits, laughing.

'Petrified,' Lexie agrees.

'Scared stupid,' Romy chips in.

And then Jake laughs, a big hearty laugh that wipes the crackle of tension clean away, and we're all laughing, big, ungainly whoops of laughter that have us clutching each other madly. I'm not alone after all – my friends feel the same. We all have doubts, we all have fears . . . we're all in it together.

'Come back at the weekend!' the waiter with the pocket watch calls as we mooch towards the door. 'We'll have a new batch of healthy cakes in. Wheatgrass, goji berry and crunchy kale flapjacks!'

'Sure,' Lexie says, polite as ever.

But of course by Saturday we'll be in Devon.

73

We split up, the others heading into town to pick up last-minute bits and pieces for the trip. I make an excuse and head for home and Jake tags along.

'Tell your parents,' he says, the moment we're alone. 'They'll know what to do. It could be something really simple, something they can fix with vitamin pills, or a sun lamp or a steady supply of hot chocolate and raw vegan cupcakes.'

'If only . . .'

'Tell your parents,' Jake pushes. 'Please?'

I allow the thought to flicker across my mind. Is Jake right? Could I tell them? I am so weary of keeping all this to myself.

'Maybe,' I concede at last.

'Definitely maybe.'

Jake drops a wrapped chocolate lime into my blazer pocket, smiles and walks away.

SashaSometimes

178 likes

SashaSometimes Packing . . .

Kezsez07 First like!

littlejen Ooh, holiday?

Tilly08 Where d'you get the cute hat?

Brownie Off on tour?

SaraLou Tell us more!

MattBFotos Cannot wait!

9

Nothing to Worry About

It's such a long time since I've heard raised voices at home that I almost don't recognize the sound of my parents, angry, yelling.

'This whole thing is stupid!' my dad says. 'Can't you see that? Why do you never listen to me?'

'Because sometimes you're wrong!' Mum's voice blazes. 'Why can't you just trust me? You always have to think the worst –'

My key turns in the lock and I step into the hallway. The raised voices halt at once and my parents' shocked faces stare at me from the open-plan kitchen. Dad's fists are clenched and Mum looks like she's been crying.

Panic flares inside me.

'Oh, hello, pet,' Mum says, as if she's doing nothing more unusual than unpacking the shopping. 'Fancy omelette for tea? Ice cream for afters?'

'Why were you shouting?' I ask.

'We weren't shouting,' Dad says with a frown. 'Just . . . discussing something.'

'Nothing to worry about,' Mum adds.

I don't believe them. I'd let myself imagine coming home, sitting down at the kitchen table, finding the words to tell my parents there was something wrong, that I was zoning out several times a day and terrified that I couldn't hide it any longer.

Instead, I'd walked right into the kind of row I thought was ancient history.

The air still crackles with tension, and I watch as my dad picks up his keys.

'I'm heading back up to the site,' he says gruffly. 'Got some paperwork to do, and I want to check everything's been left OK. See you later.'

'Wait –' my mum begins, but Dad's gone, the front door clicking firmly shut behind him.

'Mum?' I say. 'What's wrong?'

She turns to face me, eyes bright, smile only a little wobbly. 'Nothing's wrong, Sash, I promise you! Everything's fine – more than fine! So . . . omelette? Give me half an hour and it'll be on the table. Have you got homework?'

'Always,' I say. 'I guess I'll get it out of the way . . .'

In my room, I kick off my still-damp shoes and socks, hang my blazer on the radiator. My hands are shaking and there's a barbed-wire knot of anxiety in my gut.

My parents are fighting again.

Is it money troubles as I thought the other day? Is someone ill? Is something wrong at work? What has made Dad so angry with Mum, made her think he doesn't trust her? I don't know.

I can't share my troubles with them now . . . the last thing they need is me adding to the problem. I need to smooth things out, keep up the pretence that everything's fine – for now at least.

Maybe I can sort this on my own? Jake's right, I need to know exactly what's going on. I pick up my phone and click through to Google. What do I look up, though? Black holes? Vanishing? Blackouts?

I type in 'zone-out moments', then falter as a list of results pops up. Do I really want to know? I click on one link and see the words *stress, anxiety, depression.* Zoning out can be the mind's way to retreat from stressful situations, the website says. It's a mental health issue.

Tears blur my eyes and the weight of shame and sadness presses down a little more heavily on my shoulders. Anxiety, stress, depression . . . it all fits. First my parents rowing, now this? My head can't process it.

I draw in a deep breath and click away to Instagram, my happy place.

The relief is instant. Now I'm distracted by new likes and comments, the panic recedes. Jake was wrong – knowing more about the problem can only make me feel worse. My only chance of coping is to blank it, get through it, keep trying.

I will not own those words – depression, anxiety. I will not. I push the whole idea away, so far away I can barely see it. Denial is what I'm good at, right?

Forcing a smile on to my face, I haul out the little vintage suitcase that sits beside my dressing table, keeping my make-up and hair stuff tidy. It's not the case I'm taking to

Devon, but it looks good, and I busy myself styling a new image for my Instagram feed, a few pretty scarves and bright tops spilling out artfully. I take my time, make sure I get the right angle, spend a while choosing the best frame and filter and then I post it.

There's an almost instant reward as the likes and comments begin to flood in, and then my phone beeps with a text from Romy.

> Hey Sash, u busy? Bought a
> couple of things in town but not
> sure of them. Can I come show
> u? R x

I text back quickly telling her to head over, and by the time I've checked my Instagram feed again and gone down to tell Mum, Romy's at the door. I feel stronger now, brighter. So what if I'm patched together with denial and Instagram likes? It's better than falling apart.

The three of us have omelette and salad for dinner. Mum quizzes us about the Devon trip and tries to stay upbeat,

but I can see she's struggling. Afterwards Romy and I wash the dishes and head upstairs.

'Where's your dad tonight?' Romy asks casually.

'Working late. He and Mum were having a row when I got in – not sure what it was about.'

Romy frowns. 'Everyone argues, don't they? They'd tell you if it was anything serious.'

Would they? I'm not sure.

'Your parents are cool,' Romy says staunchly. 'And if they are going through a funny patch – well, you're away next week, aren't you? Maybe it'll give them some space to work things through?'

I bite my lip. 'You think so?'

'I know so,' Romy says. 'Stop worrying!'

I can't help laughing. If Romy knew what a mess my head was right now, she'd never believe it.

We've talked endlessly about magazines and clothes and boys and music. We've even talked about stage fright, compared notes, tried to help each other. I could tell her about the zone-out moments, the fear, even the stuff I saw on the internet. I know she'd listen, I know she'd care, I know she'd never judge. But is it fair to stress her out when she already has so much on her plate?

I should be supporting her, not the other way round.

'How d'you feel about leaving your mum this week?' I ask, trying to be the good friend I know I should be. 'Are you OK about it?'

Romy shrugs. 'I think so. Mum's cousin Maggie arrived yesterday, and we've gone through all the routines, all the stuff she might need to know. Mum's fairly well just now, so . . . it should be fine! To be honest, she's so excited about the whole idea of us going to record with Ked Wilder that I don't think it was ever an option for me not to go.'

I grin. 'My parents are the same,' I confess. 'I just hope . . . well, I don't want to let the band down!'

'You won't let anyone down,' Romy says. 'I know how you feel. I still get terrible nerves when we perform in front of an audience, but you told me to act confident, look the part – and that helps. I'm better than I used to be. And nobody would ever guess you were nervous. You look every inch the star!'

'I don't feel that way.'

'You hide it well,' Romy promises.

82

She's right, but I'm not sure how much longer I can keep up the facade.

Romy nudges me. 'The other thing you're hiding well is whatever's going on with you and Matt Brennan,' she teases. 'Go on, spill . . . has he asked you out yet?'

'Why is everyone so fixated on me and Matt Brennan?' I exclaim, faking outrage. 'We're just friends, that's all. Jake was practically warning me off him earlier. I mean – what the heck? It's none of his business at all!'

Romy raises an eyebrow. 'Yeah, but Jake has a thing for you himself, doesn't he?' she says. 'Don't be too hard on him.'

I blink. 'Huh? Jake? I don't know what you're talking about!'

'You must have noticed,' she says. 'He goes all mushy when you're around!'

'He doesn't! Does he?'

Romy grins. 'He's really nice, Sasha. Funny and kind. But I do sort of see the attraction of Matt Brennan's quiff.'

'Matt's so good-looking,' I sigh. 'A bit too good-looking, almost. And he's really easy to talk to and so talented . . .'

83

Romy's eyes shine. 'I bet something happens while we're in Devon,' she says. 'A kiss, maybe? Your first kiss! He's going to ask you out – I just know it! The question is, who will you pick? Matt or Jake?'

I roll my eyes. I like Jake a lot, but he's no match for Matt Brennan. Then again, neither am I – if Matt ever did ask me out, I'd be way out of my depth. But also on cloud nine . . .

'What about you?' I ask. 'Any romance in the air?'

Romy blushes. 'Not really. I mean, you know I quite like George . . . but he never really notices me. Maybe this week will change that? I want to look my best – can I show you what I bought?' From her bag, Romy pulls out a baggy jumper and a red plaid shirt big enough to fit my dad. 'I wish you'd been there to help me choose. The assistant said these were perfect for a curvy shape, but I'm not sure. I don't want to look frumpy and dull.'

'Oh, Romy! You're not frumpy, not one bit . . . but I'm not sure the shop assistant gave you great advice. These tops are huge!'

Romy shrugs. 'So am I!'

'You are not!' I argue. 'You're so hard on yourself . . . there's nothing wrong with your figure at all. So you've got curves – good! You look amazing. But you don't need to follow other people's rules and hide under shapeless layers!'

'Easy for you to say,' Romy says with a sigh.

'Oh, Romy, that's not true! I'm a million miles from perfect – you know that more than anyone. It's all about confidence and attitude – and if you don't feel confident, acting like you do can help. That's all any of us do! Pick out the clothes that flatter, use a bit of make-up maybe. Seriously . . . make the most of what you've got!'

I pull out a drawer and throw a couple of T-shirts and a miniskirt in black stretchy fabric at my friend. Romy is bigger than me but not as tall, and I'm willing to bet some of my stuff will fit her.

Romy, bemused, tries on a black T-shirt with the miniskirt, but she can't bear to look in the mirror until I let her layer the red plaid shirt on top. It looks amazing.

'I look . . . I dunno, I look OK!' she says, astonished.

I grin. 'See? You look great,' I tell her. 'That jumper will look great with the miniskirt too! Honestly, Romy, you're beautiful – a proper hourglass shape. Hang on – that's given me an idea!'

I rummage through the back of my wardrobe and pull out a vintage fifties dress that once belonged to my gran. She gave it to me for a fancy-dress party last year, but the bright, busy print and the cinched-in waist didn't suit me.

They suit Romy all right – she looks incredible.

'Borrow this lot for Devon,' I say. 'George won't know what's hit him!'

Romy gives a little twirl, her face bright with excitement, 'OK, Sasha – you next for the makeover treatment!' she says.

Her taste is a little more out there than mine, and I'm prancing about in an old polka-dot onesie with a tiara in my hair when Mum knocks gently on the door to tell us that Maggie, the Scottish cousin, has arrived to drive Romy home.

'Aww – we never got to play with the make-up,' I say.

'Next time,' Romy says. 'Thanks, Sash. For the clothes, and . . . well, everything!' She sheds the floppy hat and feather boa she's been wearing, picks up her bag and runs out to the car.

'Looks like you two've been having fun,' Mum says, as we wave Romy off. 'Sorry to cut it short. We could still play with make-up, if you like?'

So that's what we do, Mum dabbing and painting and stroking my face with colour, the way she has so many times before. I let go, relax – and when I open my eyes again I can see she's painted dramatic zebra stripes on my eyelids and fake beauty spots shaped like little black hearts.

I throw my arms round Mum, laughing, but I suddenly notice dark shadows under her eyes I've never noticed before. She has looked tired and washed-out these last few weeks I realize. If I hadn't been so wrapped up in myself, I'd have noticed sooner.

Something's wrong.

'Mum . . . you would tell me, wouldn't you? If anything was up?'

She sighs. 'Nothing to worry about, pet. Honestly . . . nothing at all.'

L&F trip

KedWilder; SashaSometimes; LexieLawlor; HappiA; SamiTagara; JCooke; MarleyHayes; DylanHayes; GeorgeClark; RomyT; LeeMac; BexIsBest; MattBrennan

KedWilder: Last-Minute Checklist! Hope you're all packed and ready. Just a reminder to make sure you've got all the essentials: clothes, shoes, a towel, a swimsuit, toiletries, toothbrush, medication and anything else you may want or need – within reason. (Lexie, I got your email and yes of course you can bring your tortoise!) Be sure to pack your musical instruments along with your talent, ambition and potential – you'll be needing them all. I forgot to ask if anyone has special dietary requirements but we can cater for most needs. Buzz me a message if there's something we should know. The minibus will be at Greystones at midday on Friday, so don't be late. I'll see you tomorrow night!

MarleyHayes: Can't wait!

MattBrennan: Can't believe this awesome opportunity!

LexieLawlor: We'll be there, don't worry!

SashaSometimes left the conversation

10

Fox Hollow Hall

The minibus sweeps to a halt in front of an imposing sandstone mansion draped in ivy and late-flowering roses. This is Fox Hollow Hall, Ked Wilder's home in Devon – and our home too for the next few days. I take in a deep breath.

'Here we are!' the driver calls out. His name is Mike, and he lives here – he used to be one of Ked Wilder's roadies, but now he works in Ked's studio and sometimes helps out as a driver. 'Everybody out! I'll open the back and you can get your luggage.'

My feet crunch on thick gravel and I set down my shoulder bag and stretch. Four hours in a minibus gets kind

of tiring, even when you've spent part of it sitting next to a cute Year Eleven boy with a wayward quiff and a ready supply of conversation, big dreams and a family-sized bag of cheese and onion crisps.

'Wow,' Matt says. 'This place . . . it's incredible!'

'Like a palace,' Romy agrees.

'Whaddya think, Mary Shelley?' Lexie asks, lifting her pet tortoise out of her carrying case. 'This is home for the next few days! Awesome, huh?'

The little tortoise gazes up at Fox Hollow Hall, awed and silent – I know how she feels. I'm used to the fading grandeur of Louisa Winter's house, but this place is something else. Every window gleams, every climbing rose is neatly pruned . . . even the gravel has been raked to a perfect thickness. Just ahead of us, Ked Wilder's vintage red Triumph Spitfire is parked rakishly, the bodywork buffed to a high shine. To one side of the main house, a huge, ornate conservatory leans against the building, and I can see flashes of turquoise water and tall tropical plants inside.

A swimming pool!

The fear inside me stills and fades, replaced by the fizz of excitement and hope.

'It really is amazing!' I exclaim, hauling my suitcase from the minibus. 'Like another world – I can't quite believe it!'

'Believe it,' Matt replies. 'It's another world all right, and we're part of it – for a few days, anyhow. How cool is that?'

He steps back a couple of paces, raising his camera to capture shots of us grappling with rucksacks, cases and instruments.

'Look at the camera,' Marley instructs. 'Big grins! C'mon, people!'

We cluster together, pushing and shoving and laughing, a motley crew of misfit kids who've somehow found themselves in music industry heaven.

'You're here!'

Ked Wilder is standing in the grand entrance to Fox Hollow Hall, casual in black jeans, T-shirt and Converse, his arms stretched out in welcome. 'Come in, come in. Camille has organized tea and cake for everyone. We'll feed you up, then give you the guided tour!'

Lexie and Bex's foster parents, Mandy and Jon, bound up the steps to shake Ked's hand and explain that Jake and his stepdad, Sheddie, will be arriving under their own steam shortly. Ked nods and ushers us all inside.

The dining kitchen is industrial-chic, with a giant zinc-topped table and half a dozen small, scrubbed-pine cafe tables scattered around the room with pine and metal chairs arranged informally round them. Oversized bare light bulbs hang from ceiling hooks and the cupboards seem to be made from old factory fittings.

A feast of tea, coffee, juice and home-baked cakes awaits us, and Matt raises an eyebrow at the spread. 'Not very rock 'n' roll, is it?' he whispers. 'More Famous Five. I was expecting beer bottles and TVs being thrown off balconies – a bit of scandal!'

'Shhh!' I grin. 'He'll hear you!'

Ked is introducing Camille, a statuesque woman dressed in pink skinny jeans and a floaty pink silk tunic dress, a mass of dark braids escaping from a pink print headwrap to cascade down to her waist.

'Camille and Mike live in the basement flat,' he explains. 'Mike keeps the studio running smoothly and Camille sorts just about everything else. She'll be your go-to person if you have any questions.'

'Housekeeper?' Matt whispers. Camille is about as far as it's possible to be from any Enid Blyton fantasies of a housekeeper I might have had, but her smile is as warm as the shiny scarlet Aga in the corner.

'I'm sure I know her face,' Happi says, but I think Camille has that striking, timeless look that makes you think you've known someone forever. She is probably a decade older than my mum, but she radiates energy and kindness.

We fall into a kind of happy trance, demolishing chocolate brownies and sipping home-made smoothies while the adults drink mugs of proper coffee from the kind of fancy hissy Italian machine they have in the Leaping Llama. By the time we're ready to explore, Sheddie and Jake have arrived too, parking their ramshackle van round the back.

I was worried that I might feel awkward seeing Jake again after what Romy had said about him liking me, but his grin is as warm and easy as ever. If there's any mushy stuff going on, I honestly can't see it. I let myself relax. He's just my friend, and that's exactly what I want him to be.

'I have some calls to make,' Ked is saying. 'Camille will show you around and we'll meet back here at six. I want to talk you through the schedule.'

'Can you pinch me?' Jake says into my ear as Camille leads us up the widest staircase I've ever seen, the crimson carpet so thick that every footstep leaves a little imprint. 'Is this real?'

'If not, then I think it's some kind of mass hallucination,' I say. 'Look at Marley – his tongue is practically hanging out! This has probably ramped up his ambitions about a million per cent, and let's face it, he was already pretty full-on . . .'

Marley's eyes are out on stalks, taking in the display of framed gold, silver and platinum discs that are ranged along the walls. I can tell he's imagining having his own collection one day, and Matt is busy capturing his reactions on camera.

On the first landing Camille takes us to the right. The west wing, she tells us, is reserved for guests – us, in other words. The east wing – Ked's private quarters – is out of bounds.

I think I must vanish briefly, because when I come back to myself Jake is holding my arm, quietly asking if I can hear him, and the others have gone on ahead.

'I'm OK,' I whisper. 'Don't say anything!'

He hands me a wrapped chocolate lime for sustenance.

'Doctor's when we get back,' he whispers, steering me forward to catch up with the others. The fizz of hope and excitement from earlier evaporates, replaced by shame at my zone-out and fear that I won't be able to hide what's happening, that I'll let everyone down.

I unwrap the sweet and pretend I'm fine, and hope that nobody will notice.

'There are three bedrooms here,' Camille is explaining. 'Two en-suite family rooms with an interconnecting door, and a third – a double – just next door. Mandy and Jon, if you want to take that one, the girls can share the other two. I've put the boys up on the top floor, with Mr Shedden to supervise.'

The family rooms are gorgeous, all stripped pine floorboards and oversized beds draped in fluffy duvets. Bex, Happi and Lexie take the room with three queen-sized beds and Romy and I take the smaller one, with two. We dump our luggage and instruments, help Lexie to set up a heat lamp, food and water for Mary Shelley and set the little tortoise down to explore.

Camille takes the boys up another flight to claim their space, and back downstairs she shows us the lounge, the library, the music room and the formal dining room, then the swimming pool with its plush recliners and jungle of tall, exotic plants.

Matt is drinking it all in, eyes bright, planning photo shoots and scoping out backgrounds. He confessed on the trip down that his dream is to sell some of the pictures from this week to a national newspaper or magazine. I tried to be encouraging, but I'm not sure the tabloids will be all that interested in a bunch of kids who haven't exactly hit the big time yet.

Still, Matt is super ambitious. He really comes to life when he's talking about the future, about how he wants to be an investigative reporter on one of the national newspapers or see his photographs on the covers of the top glossy magazines.

'I love that you understand, Sasha,' he'd told me earlier, as the minibus trundled through the windy Devon lanes. 'Hardly anyone I know gets it. My mates think I'm mad, wasting time on a school magazine that even half the pupils have never heard of, and my parents think I should be something sensible like a doctor or a lawyer. I mean, can you imagine?'

He'd made a kind of tortured face, as if his parents had suggested a career in sewage maintenance or gravedigging, and I did my best to look sympathetic.

'I just don't want to settle for an ordinary life, you know?' he'd said earnestly. 'I'm destined for bigger things. I want to be the kind of journalist who exposes wrongdoing and digs for the truth no matter what. I want to take photographs that change the world, challenge the status quo – there's a fire inside me, driving me on. You understand me, Sasha. You've got that same passion and ambition yourself, after all, for music!'

I didn't have the heart to tell him he was wrong, that an ordinary life was exactly what I wanted, or at least one without the fear of letting people down constantly gnawing at my belly. Shamefully, I'd even zoned out a couple of times while Matt was talking, but luckily he'd been too wrapped up in sharing his hopes and dreams to notice. I didn't mind – I admire enthusiasm in a person, and yes, OK, I admit that I admire Matt in other ways too. Just sitting watching him talk was quite cool.

Right now, he's loping on ahead as we trek across the huge, dipping lawn, Camille explaining that the hollow is carpeted in snowdrops in February and bluebells in May, then poppies and cornflowers in high summer.

'You can spot foxes pretty much all year round,' she explains. 'But they're shy, of course, so perhaps they'll stay out of your way. Now this is the famous Fox Hollow Studios, where you'll be spending a lot of time these next few days. Take a look.'

The studio annexe is a specially designed set of buildings equipped with the best modern recording technology. Dylan can't resist trying out the shiny new drum kit – Ked had told him it would be crazy to attempt to transport his own battered kit here, and it's not hard to see that this kit is top of the range. Marley is in his element, checking everything out, but it scares me a little to see the mics and amps and the high-tech mixing desk.

'Ked has a great sound crew,' Camille tells us. 'The best in the business – but you'll find that out yourselves soon enough! I think I've shown you everything, but if you need me I'll either be in the kitchen or in the basement flat. Come and find me – I'll be happy to help. Now, I'll leave you to get back and freshen up or relax after the long drive. We have a buffet supper all ready to go in the kitchen-diner shortly, and I know Ked wants to welcome you all properly. See you at six!'

'Perfect,' Matt says, polite as ever.

Mandy, Jon, Sheddie and the Lost & Found chime in with their assent, but the wink Matt gives me is mine alone.

Friday:	Arrive, welcome, settle in, dinner
Saturday:	7 a.m. breakfast/free time
	10 a.m. Sasha vocal coaching with Camille (music room, main house), everyone else studio practice
	11 a.m. Marley, Lexie, Romy vocal coaching with Camille (backing vocals and harmonies)
	1 p.m. lunch
	2 p.m. songwriting workshop with Ked (music room, main house)
	4.30 p.m. free time
	6 p.m. dinner
	7 p.m. X Factor evening
Sunday:	7 a.m. breakfast/free time
	9 a.m. minibus to Starshine Festival, Arena Village, Bristol
	11 a.m. arrive, free time
	1–4 p.m. lunch and meetings
	4–midnight free time
	Midnight minibus to Fox Hollow Hall
Monday:	7 a.m. breakfast/free time
	9 a.m. Sasha vocal coaching with Camille
	10 a.m. whole band developing new songs with Ked and Camille (studio)
	1 p.m. lunch
	2 p.m. practising/developing new songs (studio)

4.30 p.m. Sasha, Romy, Lexie, Marley,
Sasha developing harmonies with
Camille (music room)
6 p.m. dinner
7 p.m. planning video/publicity

Tuesday: 7 a.m. breakfast/free time
9 a.m. Sasha vocal coaching with
Camille
10 a.m. make-up and styling with Ria
and Fitz
12.30 p.m. photo shoot with Matt
1.15 p.m. lunch
2 p.m. band practice/recording
4.30 p.m. free time
6 p.m. dinner
7 p.m. meeting with OK Film team to
finalize ideas

Wednesday: 7 a.m. breakfast/free time
9 a.m. Sasha vocal coaching with
Camille
10 a.m. recording
1 p.m. lunch
2 p.m. recording
4.30 p.m. free time
6 p.m. dinner with Lola Rockett
7 p.m. live set
8 p.m. free time

Thursday: 7 a.m. breakfast/free time
             9 a.m. Sasha vocal coaching with Camille
             10 a.m. Ria and Fitz, styling
             1 p.m. light lunch
             2 p.m. shoot video with OK Film
             4.30 p.m. free time
             6 p.m. dinner
             7 p.m. last-chance recording, mentoring,
             packing
Friday: 7 a.m. breakfast/packing
             10 a.m. minibus departs

Jake: shadow tech team where possible, Mike to direct
Matt: fit photos and interviews around this schedule;
check all images/copy that include mentions/shots
of Ked Wilder with Ked, Camille or Mike before use
One-to-one mentoring: all band members will be offered
a one-to-one mentoring slot with Ked and/or Camille,
at a time to suit
Mandy, Jon, Sheddie: you're here to keep an eye on the
kids, so feel free to slot in and out of sessions as you see
best – and make good use of the facilities, of course!

Ked Wilder

Ked Wilder

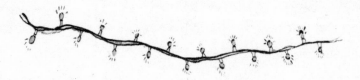

11

The Plan

The zinc-topped table holds a feast, and we fall on it as if we haven't eaten in days. It looks like all our meals will follow this informal buffet-style pattern, and Matt sticks to my side, chatting easily, loading my plate with things he thinks I will like. I'd rather pick my own food, but I know he's only trying to be nice.

'Hey, you could be a professional chef, Camille,' Marley calls out, holding up a forkful of quiche. 'I mean, you're not just a pretty face – you're a kitchen goddess! This is amazing!'

'I'm not the cook,' Camille says, frowning slightly. 'Mrs B lives in the village. She made this, but she had to leave

early today because her husband has the flu. You'll meet her tomorrow.'

I get the impression that Marley's famous charm is not quite working on Camille . . . not yet, anyway.

Once we've eaten, Ked ushers us through to the big living room, and Matt steers me towards a club chair upholstered in what looks like old hessian sacks, some printed with vintage logos and lettering. It's big enough for two, but still, I'm torn between the thrill of this and an irrational wish to be across the room, where Romy, Jake, Lexie, Sami, Happi and Bex are jostling and laughing on a sofa made from squashy cushions piled up on rough wooden pallets threaded through with fairy lights. I'm starting to believe that Matt really does like me and the idea panics me just a little.

The others grab the remaining chairs or loll on thick sheepskins in front of a roaring wood burner that makes everything feel toasty, and then Mike and Camille join us, Camille with a stack of papers in her hands.

'So – welcome to Fox Hollow Hall, people!' Ked says. 'I'm excited to be working with you this week, and happy that every single one of the Lost & Found has made the

effort to be here. It shows how keen and determined you all are, and that's half the battle! I'm grateful too, to the adults who've come along to keep an eye on you – Mandy, Jon, Sheddie, make yourselves at home. The kids will be busy this week, but you guys can chill a little as long as you're keeping an eye on them as well!'

Sheddie, sitting on the floor with his legs folded up like some kind of origami project, waves an arm in the air.

'I thought I'd do my yoga routine every morning on the grass outside,' he says, smiling. 'It's supposed to stay dry. Eightish? A few basic stretches and a Salute to the Sun sequence. Anyone who wants to join me is very welcome!'

Ked grins. 'Might take you up on that,' he says. 'Thanks! A special welcome to Jake and Matt – not members of the band, strictly speaking, but you guys already know that a band is much more than its members. I think Jake will get a lot out of shadowing my sound crew this week. Mike will be your line manager, OK? There's a lot he can teach you, and he'll certainly keep you busy.'

'OK!' Jake says, his cheeks pink with pleasure.

'And, Matt,' Ked continues. 'A late addition to the party, but welcome, of course! Having a budding photojournalist

on the team is great – dip in and out of what's going on as you wish, and feel free to arrange formal photo shoots as long as they don't overlap with anything already scheduled. It goes without saying that you're here solely to cover what's happening with the Lost & Found – please respect my privacy and that of my friends. If you're not sure about something, I'd rather you checked your copy and photos with me. I don't talk much to the press these days, and when I do it's on my terms. Understood?'

'Understood, Mr Wilder!' Matt says, bright-eyed and earnest. 'It's an absolute privilege to be here. No way would I tread on anybody's toes or report anything that isn't strictly to do with the band. I totally understand the whole privacy thing. No problem! I mean, you really don't need to worry about me, I'm just a kid with a camera who helps out on the school magazine . . .'

I can't help smiling. Matt's falling over himself to say the right thing and overdoing it slightly, but I like that he's trying so hard to please Ked Wilder.

Matt turns to me and winks. 'Bit full of himself, isn't he?' he whispers in my ear. 'As if I'd be interested in taking photos of him anyway!'

I blink, surprised at this. It seems Matt's the kind of boy who doesn't like being told what to do; underneath the smooth patter he's a little bit snarky. Not quite the perfect boy-next-door type I had him down as, then.

'These privacy rules apply to everyone here, of course,' Ked is saying. 'I'm trusting you all not to let me down.'

Matt gives a subtle eye-roll, but there's a rush of promises from everybody else. Ked smiles and goes on.

'Now – the rest of you! You know you're here because I think you have something special. I can't promise anything – the music business isn't like that . . . it's fickle and feckless and it can change in a heartbeat, so nothing is ever a sure thing. Still, I like the Lost & Found a lot, and I will do my best to help you. I'm trying to cram a lot of stuff into six short days, so I've made a plan.'

Camille jumps up and starts handing out papers. Everyone gets a copy, even the adults. Ked wasn't joking when he said there was lots to do. This schedule is kind of daunting, but – Sunday at Starshine Festival? A buzz of excitement spreads around the room.

'Starshine Festival?' Marley bursts out. 'Are you kidding me?'

'Are we playing?' Bex asks, alarmed. 'I mean, that would be awesome, but . . . I . . . are we ready for that?'

Ked laughs. 'You're not playing,' he says. 'Not because I don't think you're ready – but because it'll be fun and because I want you to meet some friends who'll be working with us next week. Starshine is one of the biggest music festivals of the year – but it's not just a festival. It's an expo, a showcase, a chance for breaking bands and top music biz and media people to get together. There'll be live music, lectures, interviews, workshops, stylists, film-makers, agents, TV people – every kind of contact you could possibly want. It's all inside, in one of the UK's biggest indoor exhibition centres – an expo village, really. There's nothing else quite like it. So that's our Sunday. Lots of fun and some useful meetings too – OK?'

Bex grins. 'OK!'

Glancing back at the schedule, I can't help noticing that I have daily voice coaching with Camille. Does that mean they're worried about me? Has Ked picked me out as the Lost & Found's weak link, someone who needs extra support? Anxiety floods through me.

Singing into your hairbrush in front of the mirror and singing in front of an audience are two very different things, and the pressure is about to get a whole lot worse.

'Sasha and some of the rest of us have vocal coaching with Camille,' Marley says, looking across at her. 'Um . . . cool, I guess, but why Camille? How come?'

'Because I'm a trained vocal coach,' she explains patiently. 'I used to sing professionally.'

Happi opens her eyes wide. 'Hang on,' she says. 'You . . . you're Camille Akinsulire, aren't you? I thought I knew your face! You used to sing with Ked back in the day, and you did backing vocals for Bowie and George Michael and Paul Weller. I mean, loads of famous people! I've seen you on YouTube!'

'YouTube?' Marley echoes. 'You're *that* Camille? Wow! I read about you in Ked's biography!'

Camille just shrugs.

'Never jump to conclusions in this business,' Ked advises. 'Or in this life, come to that. Treat everyone with respect. Camille met Mike – he was one of my roadies – on one of our tours a few decades back. I stopped touring, they settled down and had kids, and when I bought this place I asked if they'd help me run it. Camille's definitely not just a pretty face – or even just a kitchen goddess. She's the best backing singer I've ever met, and a much sought-after vocal coach in the profession.'

'OK,' Marley agrees, chastened. 'Arghhh . . . me and my big mouth! Sorry, Camille. I'm an idiot!'

'He really is,' Lee confirms. 'You kind of get used to it, after a while . . .'

Camille laughs and the tension ebbs away.

'Anyway, a singer can benefit hugely from learning good breathing and vocal techniques,' Ked says. 'It helps to protect the vocal cords. Camille can help you with harmonies too.'

I relax. So the vocal coaching is not because I'm awful . . . it's because singers need to look after their voices.

'I'll be asking a few friends in throughout the week,' Ked continues. 'Experts in their field – people whose opinions I trust. I'll be helping you with new song ideas, and you'll be working with top sound engineers to record those songs. I've asked along a make-up artist and stylist to pull together an image for the band, and OK Film, a young film crew whose work I love, will be creating a promo video for you.

On Wednesday a good friend of mine with lots of contacts in radio and TV will be having dinner with us, and I thought I'd ask you to do a short live set afterwards – I want to see what kind of an impression you make on her.'

'Lola Rockett!' Lexie says, reading her schedule. 'No way! She's my favourite radio DJ!'

'We always watch her New Year TV show,' Lexie's stepdad Jon chips in.

'You and half the people in the UK,' Ked says with a smile. 'If she likes the Lost & Found – well, I don't have to tell you what that could mean. She has a reputation for spotting tomorrow's talent, so let's hope you make a good impression!'

'We will,' Marley vows. 'I may be an idiot, but I care about the Lost & Found more than I care about anything. These kids are brilliant . . . really talented and awash with star quality.'

Ked rakes a hand through his grey-blond hair and smiles.

'Let's just say you're a band with potential,' he says. 'I don't see that very often these days, and I think we can make something of it, but only if you're willing to work. You talk a good story, Marley, but I'm looking for more

than words here. Talent? Well, that's ten a penny – you can find it all around you. Brilliance? I'm not seeing it yet. Star quality? Who knows? It's way too soon to say.'

Marley looks shell-shocked, as if Ked has just smashed his dreams to pieces, and I shiver in spite of the wood burner, aware of how much is at stake over the coming days. Everyone is looking serious now, shaken by Ked's appraisal. Do we have what it takes?

Do I?

'Don't look so scared,' Ked says, laughing. 'I'm not asking for perfection – that doesn't exist – but this week we'll do things differently. You don't need a keyboardist, for starters – you have so many rich layers of sound already, and Sasha should be focusing on her strength – vocals.'

I blink, pleased at the compliment. Ditching the keyboards means one less thing to worry about, which has to be good.

'Right,' he finishes. 'I need you to give your absolute best. I'm looking for hard graft and the ability to take criticism and learn from it without falling apart. I'm giving you a chance here, a big chance – but you have to want it, and you have to work for it. Don't let me down!'

Ked has turned the mood of the room around, pulled us all together, whipped up a tide of determination and solidarity.

'We won't!' my band mates insist, and although I smile and move my lips, I can't bring myself to say the words out loud. It's a promise I'm not sure I can keep.

Hope you got there safely! I expect they've kept you busy, but if you do get a minute, give us a call so I know all is well! Thinking of you living the high life while we're eating microwave ready-meals in front of Bake Off! Mum & Dad x

Sorry! Only just seen this – I'm sharing a room and Romy's asleep now. I'll call tomorrow. All is well. There's so much planned I think going back to school will be a holiday after this! Sash x

So excited for you. Was hoping you'd check in before I fell asleep! Your dad's gone up now – he has an early start. Wish I could be there with you. Talk to Mandy if there's anything at all worrying you, and promise you'll keep us in the loop! Mum x

Promise! This place is amazing! Gold taps in the en-suite and an actual swimming pool! Better try to sleep now. Big day tomorrow! Love you! Sash x

Love you more – Mum x

12

The Picnic

I can't sleep, tossing and turning, my mind running on
endless loops of what might go wrong. I finally fall asleep
just before dawn, but the faint aroma of warm croissants
and coffee pull me to consciousness as the morning light
begins to filter through the curtains. I yawn and stretch,
determined to grab another hour of sleep, then almost
jump out of my skin as I see Matt peering round the
bedroom door, his quiff all rumpled and fluffy, grinning
at me.

I sit up in a panic, pulling the duvet round me.

'What are you *doing*?' I hiss. 'You're not allowed in here!'

'Huh? Who? What?' Romy grumbles from the other side of the room, rubbing her eyes. She blinks at Matt and then dives back under the covers. 'Noooo . . . go away!'

'I come in peace,' Matt says. 'Honest! Just wondered if you wanted to come for a breakfast picnic.'

'We don't!' growls Romy's muffled voice, but I think Matt's invitation is aimed at me and, even though I'm still tired and wary, it makes me smile.

'Give me five minutes,' I tell him. 'Ten, maybe. I'll meet you in the kitchen . . . now go! You're not even supposed to be on this floor – Mandy and Jon will go mad if they find you!'

Matt just laughs and backs out, the door closing softly behind him.

I jump up and sprint to the en-suite bathroom and take the fastest shower of my life before pulling on black skinny jeans and a cute T-shirt. I blast my hair with the hairdryer (more groaning from Romy) and carefully do my face, applying some low-key eyeshadow and a couple of flicks of liner.

'You'll freeze,' Romy comments, huddled in her duvet. 'A picnic at the end of October?'

'Why not?' I dig out a fluffy jumper from the suitcase, pulling it on and checking in the mirror. The deep blue picks out the colour of my eyes and Romy grins and gives me the thumbs up.

I'm downstairs in fifteen minutes, which is a record for me, but Matt laughs and points at his watch.

'What kept you?' he asks. 'I've been up since six. Had a swim and fancied some company for breakfast . . . you could have just come down in your pyjamas!'

'In someone else's house? Not a chance!'

'You were worth waiting for,' he says. 'C'mon, let's grab some food!'

A plump middle-aged woman, who's much closer to my idea of a housekeeper than Camille, is setting out a breakfast spread of pastries, cheese, fruit and yoghurt. On a side counter the fancy coffee machine is bubbling away and there are four different sorts of fruit juice to choose from.

'Mrs B?' Matt says, putting on the charm. 'We've heard so much about you! Fresh croissants . . . and are those warm pain au chocolat? Can we take a few bits and pieces outside for a breakfast picnic? This place is amazing and we don't want to miss a single thing.'

'Of course!'

Mrs B ends up packing us a picnic basket of pastries, fruit and cheese, with a carton of fresh orange juice and two checked napkins.

'Ready?' Matt grins. 'Follow me!'

We head out through the back door, Matt leading the way towards a copse of trees to one side of the house. We crunch our way through fallen leaves, gold and russet and burnt orange, and stop at a clearing where ivy and wild honeysuckle twines upward into the trees. It's so pretty it takes my breath away.

Matt hands me a croissant, and the minute I bite into it he raises his camera and captures a few frames of me with flakes of warm pastry on my chin.

'Cute pictures,' he says, scanning the screen.

I blink. Does that mean he thinks I'm cute? Or just ridiculous, with flakes of croissant round my mouth? I can't tell.

'It's cool here, huh?' Matt says, sitting down on a fallen tree trunk. 'And great for spotting wildlife too. Can you see what I see? What species of tree d'you think they are?'

He takes my arm and steers me round until I'm looking past the woodland and out towards the grass beyond. My eyes widen as I see Sheddie leading the yoga class he mentioned last night. Ked, Camille, Mandy, Jon and – unexpectedly – Marley, are all balanced on one leg, arms above their head in prayer position. They look comical, Ked especially, as he's wearing baggy Indian yoga pants and a headband instead of his trademark skinny jeans and black fedora.

I know they're doing the Tree Pose because Mum used to go to yoga classes and she practised it in the living room sometimes, while watching *EastEnders*.

Matt starts fiddling with his camera, attaching some kind of zoom lens. I watch as he raises his camera, training it on the yoga class. This is exactly what Ked warned him about last night, surely?

'Umm . . . Matt . . . I don't think . . .'

'Shhh,' he whispers. 'They can't see us and it's too good to miss!'

But Ked must have superhuman hearing, because at that moment, just as the rest of the group move smoothly out of the Tree Pose and into the Downward Dog, he looks across and frowns in our direction.

118

'Matt?' he calls. 'What are you doing?'

Matt steps out of the trees so that Ked and the yoga group can see him clearly.

'I'm having a breakfast picnic with Sasha,' he says brightly. 'We noticed the yoga class, and then I spotted a fox skulking across the grass behind you. I didn't think – I just wanted to capture the moment!'

Ked looks around, but of course there is no fox. There never was a fox – I'm pretty sure of that.

'He's gone,' Matt says with a shrug. 'No worries. I'll get a shot if it's the last thing I do. I love wildlife! Sorry if I put you off your stride . . . I wasn't focused on you guys. I've got the zoom lens on – I was looking way past you!'

'OK,' Ked says. 'Perhaps look for your fox picture once the class is over?'

'No problem, Mr Wilder,' Matt says. 'Whatever you say!' He waves and steps back into the trees, sinks down again on the tree trunk and bites into an apple.

'Was there a fox?' I ask, bemused.

'As if!' Matt says, taking off the zoom lens and packing it away.

My eyes widen. 'You didn't . . . take pictures of Ked? What about our promise to respect his privacy?'

Matt rolls his eyes. 'It's not like I'm going to *do* anything with them,' he says. 'It was just funny, that's all. What's the harm?'

'I don't know. It's just that Ked said . . .'

'Ked's paranoid,' Matt scoffs. 'He thinks everything's about him, but actually he's yesterday's news, just an old bloke in baggy trousers standing on one leg. Don't worry, Sasha. It was a laugh!'

I bite my lip.

'Will you delete the pictures?' I ask. 'Please?'

Matt laughs. 'Seriously? You're worse than he is! OK, fine – I'll delete them.' He looks down at the camera, swipes and clicks and looks up again, grinning. 'Happy now? C'mon. Lighten up! I didn't come here to take pictures of a wrinkly old has-been. I wanted to do some portrait shots of the beautiful lead singer of an up-and-coming teen band . . .'

'Oh!'

And then I realize what he's saying, and my cheeks flare pink, my breath catching in my throat as if I've just

unwrapped the loveliest surprise present ever. Matt Brennan thinks I'm beautiful. It's the best thing that's ever happened to me – and the scariest too.

I am out of my depth with this boy. He's too slick, too cool – way, way too confident for me. He's cute and chatty and flirty, but I'm starting to see a streak of something less appealing behind it. I'm not sure I know the real Matt Brennan, not yet.

But . . . he's so good-looking, and he makes my heart beat harder than one of Dylan's drum solos.

'Just sit back against that tree – perfect,' he's saying. 'Your hair looks amazing against the ivy and the honeysuckle. Pretend I'm not here. Look over to the left . . . relax . . . that's great! You look so dreamy and a little bit sad. You're not sad, are you, Sash?'

'No!' I tell him. 'Of course not!'

'Good! OK. Look up at the branches . . . tilt your head to one side . . . awesome!'

Matt leans forward and moves a few strands of hair away from my face, at the same time tugging a strand of ivy down across my shoulder. I know I should laugh or say something witty, something cool, but I can't move, can't speak. I close

my eyes and wish I could disappear, even though I know it doesn't work that way, that I can't choose the moments when I slip away into nothingness. I wish I could because sometimes the real world feels too scary, too real.

The camera clicks away and I stay frozen, barely breathing, feeling like a butterfly, captured and pinned into a frame for all the world to see.

SashaSometimes

243 likes

SashaSometimes Wishing on a fallen leaf . . . to work with Ked Wilder on our new EP!
#Lost&Found #DreamsComeTrue #NewEP #ReachForTheStars

MillfordGirl1 Wow . . . does this mean what I think it means?

Musicismylife Yes! An EP! Finally!

littlejen You're working with Ked Wilder? For real?

CynicalTeen When will the EP be out? Cute pic btw!

KTCool U r my role model!

MattBFotos Cute

13

Just Breathe

I am a full ten minutes early for my vocal coaching lesson with Camille, and right now I feel anxious, panicky and full of dread. Camille is hugely respected in the business – I didn't know her name the way Happi did, but I Googled her and she has sung on some iconic hits, old songs I know by heart and love to bits.

Last night Romy, Lexie, Bex, Happi and I sat up watching clips on YouTube, clips that showed a younger Camille belting out backing vocals behind various pop icons. I'm in awe. She is a pop legend in her own right, and suddenly I'm worried that I won't come up to scratch. A shy, untrained teen with an awkward habit of zoning out at moments of stress . . . I'm not exactly the ideal pupil.

Camille comes into the music room, dramatic in a turquoise silk tunic and huge silver hoops in her ears. 'Morning, Sasha! Hope you slept well. So, the band's lead singer! I'm guessing you've dreamed of this your whole life, am I right?'

I squirm. Does singing in the shower count as a lifelong ambition? I don't think it does, but how can I admit that? It would feel like a huge betrayal of my band mates, and ungrateful too.

'I . . . I do like singing,' I say.

Camille grins. 'You're modest,' she says. 'That's cute! Have you had lessons before? D'you know the basics?'

I shake my head, and Camille says that's fine. She says she's not actually going to teach me to sing, because I can do that already . . . just show me ways to use my voice more safely and effectively.

'Think of it as an insurance policy for your vocal skills,' she says. 'The voice is your instrument – you don't want to strain or damage it. I'm going to show you how to use your breath to make sure the vocal cords are relaxed, because if there's any tension there, it could cause harm. I have some techniques to help you push up the volume too – safely, of course! It's all in the breathing. Let's start off with some warm-ups!'

It's hard to stay stressed and anxious when you're humming up five notes and down again, getting higher and higher all the time. Just when I'm getting the hang of it, we switch to a 'zzz' sound because Camille says it engages the abs and intercostals, whatever they might be, and then finally to an 'eee' sound because Camille says that will 'open things up' a bit.

'Now sing me a song, Sasha,' Camille instructs. 'Any song – one of the band's or an old one you like, doesn't matter. We're all warmed up – so show me what you can do! Remember your breathing – no big breaths in the middle of a phrase, no gasping, no rushing. Go!'

I'm singing 'Over the Rainbow', a song I've loved since I was little. This kind of scrutiny would have had me tied up in knots earlier, but the warm-ups have relaxed me and I trust Camille. I respect her expertise and I'm grateful for her kindness too . . . That counts for a lot.

'Ease up, Sasha,' she says, coming up behind me, resting her hands on my shoulders and gently pressing down. 'You're holding a lot of tension here – can you feel it? Keep your upper body relaxed. Just breathe: let the breath go deep into your body like a yoga breath. Good girl! It's hard work, I know, but it's worth it.'

I'm high on the buzz of knowing I've got the breathing right, but then things slide sideways. Camille is looking at me, frowning, and I know I've tuned out again, lost a chunk of time. A sheen of sweat breaks out across my forehead and my face flares with shame.

'Sasha?' she's asking. 'Is something wrong?'

'No, no . . . I'm sorry,' I say. 'Must have been dreaming!'

I won't give in. According to the internet, zone-out moments happen because of stress, anxiety and depression. I can't accept that . . . I won't. I peel off the fluffy jumper and try to carry on, but my confidence has taken a knock and I stumble my way through the next few exercises, awkward and uncertain.

'Just breathe,' Camille says again. 'You're overthinking this. Take it from the top, but this time you and I are going to play an imaginary tennis match while you're singing. Let's take the focus away from the song, see if that helps.'

'Tennis?' I echo, confused.

'Tennis,' she says. 'Let's call it kinetic distraction. Trust me, Sasha.'

She raises an imaginary tennis racquet, lobs an imaginary tennis ball towards me. Without thinking, I lob it back.

Camille laughs. 'Good! OK. Start singing – and breathe! That's it!'

Imaginary tennis somehow stops the panic pulling me down, and a few minutes in I'm singing well again, using Camille's breathing techniques to really project. It's exhilarating and it's fun – and then it happens again, the black-hole thing, and Camille is looking at me, concerned.

I haven't just dropped the ball – I've lost the game, set and match. It takes a special kind of stupid to lose at imaginary tennis.

'Camille . . . I'm sorry. I was trying my best, honest!'

'I know you were,' she tells me kindly. 'We crammed a lot in, and we'll do more tomorrow, but you've done well for a first session, I promise. You have a lovely voice, crystal clear and full of feeling. We just need to work on getting

you to relax. You're holding so much stress, sweetie – why is that?'

Tears sting my eyes and I blink them away, determined not to show weakness, not now, not here. I won't give in.

I'm not even sure how I got into this mess . . . the stuff with the band seemed to happen so fast. One minute Marley was dragging me along to audition as a uke player, the next he was telling me I should be the lead singer. I went along with it, didn't take it seriously . . . I thought it would be a bunch of kids jamming together, having fun, being friends. I thought there'd be no pressure . . . but of course it was never going to be that way, not with Marley. I sometimes think he has ambition running through his veins the way the rest of us have blood.

I've tried so hard. I walked on to the stage at the big park festival and sang my heart out, even though I felt sick, even though I was shaking all over. Nobody seemed to notice – they told me I was a natural. The crowd went wild, and that didn't seem the right moment to tell Marley I was struggling.

I haven't found the right moment since, and now I seem to be losing random chunks of my life every day, usually at

the worst possible time. The sick, anxious feelings just get worse and worse.

Camille is watching me carefully, thoughtfully. I'd like to trust her, but I don't quite dare.

I shrug. 'I'm nervous, that's all,' I say. 'I didn't sleep too well . . . and so much depends on this week, doesn't it? Maybe I panicked a bit. I thought I was getting it wrong, so I just . . . stopped.'

I don't know if this sounds plausible, but it's the best I can come up with for now.

'I'm not really at ease on stage,' I admit, throwing in something honest. 'Not like the others. I worry. I don't want to let anyone down!'

Camille sighs. 'We all get that frisson of nerves before a performance,' she says. 'It's natural – it gets the adrenaline going and helps us to pull out all the stops to create an amazing show. Most performers will tell you they're nervous beforehand – but once they step on to that stage, they forget it all and love every moment.'

'Not me,' I say. 'Not even close. Does it get any easier?'

'Some people do get bad stage fright,' she admits. 'It's certainly possible to overcome it. I'm sure we can help you,

Sasha – leave this with me. I'll have a think, and we can work on some techniques and tactics tomorrow. We can sort it!'

I feel a whole lot lighter as I walk away.

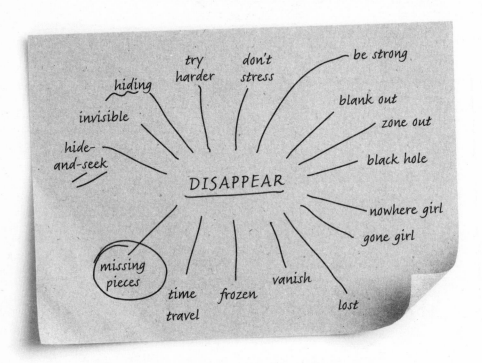

14

Song

'Are you even listening?' Matt says.

I blink and glance up at him, struggling to gather the threads of what I've missed and weave them into some kind of smokescreen to camouflage my vanishing.

We're sitting in the kitchen at lunch, a couple of plates of toasted cheese sandwiches in front of us along with two half-drunk smoothies. My band mates are scattered about the kitchen, chatting at other tables. I catch the tail end of a conversation about this morning's studio practice – Lexie and Romy singing one of the voice exercises Camille has given them, Sami sketching, Lee grumbling that he's a trumpet player and not a lyricist, so why should he have to do the songwriting workshop? No clues there.

At the back of the kitchen, Mrs B is stacking the dishwasher, wiping down the zinc-topped table. She looks weary – the way I feel.

'Sasha?' Matt prompts.

I make a guess based on Matt's favourite topic of conversation: himself, his hopes, his dreams.

'Of course I'm listening,' I bluff. 'I think I just got a bit carried away with the images you were conjuring up, that's all. You're going all the way to the top, Matt – I know you are! It's so exciting!'

Matt frowns. 'OK. It's just – you looked miles away there.'

I nod and shrug. 'I was. I was thinking . . . I mean, you're so sure of the path you're treading. It's like you know exactly where you're going – you don't doubt it for a minute. Marley's like that too, I know, but . . . I don't think I am, Matt. When I try to think of the future, it's just a blur. It scares me!'

Matt's frown clears and he's back on track again, confident and in control.

'Well, maybe you can't see it, Sasha,' he tells me. 'But everyone else can. You have shedloads of star quality! Your voice is stunning and you look . . . well, you look amazing, you must know that. You're the face of the band! Just wait, in a few months – or weeks even – your picture's going to be on the cover of the music magazines and in all the papers!'

The words are intended to reassure me, make me smile, but of course they don't. Just the opposite.

'It's a great story,' Matt pushes on. 'Teen band hit the big time! There's been nothing like this in decades . . . not these days, when new bands are put together like jigsaws by music managers with an eye for the main chance, or voted to the Christmas number-one spot after endless rounds on a reality TV show. No, the Lost & Found are different. You're right on the edge of something huge!'

I bite my lip. 'But what if that's not what I want?' I ask. 'What if I'm not ready for it? What if I never am?'

Matt laughs. 'Nobody ever feels ready for fame and fortune,' he promises me. 'Except Marley, maybe. And me!

Look, I love that you're so sweet and so shy, Sasha. Trust me, that just makes you more interesting!'

He puts out his hand and touches mine, squeezing tightly, giving me the kind of melty-eyed gaze that makes me think I might faint.

How come that when I'm given everything I thought I wanted I just panic? A shot at fame, attention from a cool boy – it's all here for the taking, but what I feel is way, way out of my depth. I'm not sweet or shy, not really – just struggling.

Matt reckons I'm not listening to him, but he doesn't even try to listen to me. Nobody does. Maybe I really am invisible?

I smile, and Matt relaxes, grins, releases my hand.

'It's going to happen,' he tells me. 'It really is! And you're going to love every bit of it, Sasha – I'll make sure of that!'

Matt Brennan may be cute, but I'm not sure I believe a word he says.

The songwriting workshop is cool. Ked tells us that it doesn't matter what we do in the band – we all have

something to offer. Inspiration is everywhere, he says, and with an open mind we can all learn to be creative.

'A band that can write their own material has a head start,' Ked declares. 'It maximizes your chances of finding a hit song, a song with magic.'

'Lexie is our lyricist,' Lee complains. 'I'm no good with words. I'm dyslexic – it's all about the music for me, not words. I couldn't write a poem – or whatever it is you want – to save my life!'

'Hey,' Ked tells him. 'This isn't a lesson in grammar, I promise you, and I couldn't care less about your spelling. All the ideas sheets we produce today will be anonymous, anyway, if you want them to be. They're starting points, that's all. I'm not looking for lyrics – just raw ideas. Imagination. Wordplay. The chances are it'll be Lexie weaving her magic with your ideas – and Marley bringing them to life with tune and melody, but this is *your* chance to contribute too!'

'Suppose I'll give it a go then,' Lee says, looking nervous.

'Good man!' Ked grins. 'OK! Take a sheet of paper and write down a word that means something to you, then create a spider chart of words or phrases you associate with that word. No rhymes, no verses, no stress! Don't take it too seriously – just see what happens.'

Marley shrugs and takes a marker pen and a blank sheet of paper from the pile. He writes the word STAR in capitals in the centre, then adds lines radiating out to other words – *fame, fortune, destiny, pop legend, gold disc, rock icon*. It's not hard to see how his mind works – it's kind of one-track, but that's OK. He's broken the ice, taken the pressure off.

The rest of us take marker pens and sheets of paper, and find somewhere to sit and think. I choose a quiet corner of the room and sit cross-legged on the stripped pine floorboards, wondering what on earth to write. When I look at the page again, I somehow know that time has slipped sideways again and for just a few moments I was somewhere else, somewhere unreachable.

Just for a moment, I disappeared.

I pick up the marker pen and write the word DISAPPEAR, and I have no problem finding more words and phrases to scatter on the page around it. When I've finished, I fold the sheet into quarters so nobody can see what I've written, and add it to the growing pile of papers on the table. It feels like an SOS signal, but hopefully in code. Nobody will have a clue what it means.

I must have missed the next instruction, because my band mates are digging into the piles of glossy magazines, cutting out words and images. I select a couple of fashion mags, a sheaf of plain paper and some glue and scissors, then retreat to my corner. Inspiration doesn't strike, and I find myself flicking through the beauty pages. Mum buys magazines like these, and both of us love reading about new products and techniques. I have a whole scrapbook at home of my favourite make-up looks.

I glance up guiltily. Lee is busily cutting and pasting; Bex is rearranging chopped-up sentences, an expression of intense concentration on her face; Sami has gone off-script and started making a collage of images and words combined.

I go back to the beauty pages, slice out a page of a beautifully made-up model, her skin satin-smooth, her lips like red velvet. What now? There are ads for face masks, for concealer, lipstick, eyeshadow, foundation, liner – and dozens and dozens of features on how to use them to best effect. There are a million different ways to make a girl look better, braver, more beautiful, to hide her flaws, her imperfections, herself.

How many ways there seem to be for a girl to hide.

I snip out a few words and phrases from the ads and articles, play around with them and finally glue them on the face of the model. It's not a song, that's for sure, and I don't think it's a poem.

It feels almost like a cry for help.

MaSk

IMPROVE SKIN TONE AND TEXTURE

FRESH NEW YOU *hide blemishes*

flawless

LOOK BETTER THAN EVER BEFORE

pretty and bright

COMPLETE COVERAGE, CONCEALS IMPERFECTIONS

banish acne, open pores, dark shadows

BLEND AND HIGHLIGHT FOR ALL-DAY
CAMERA-READY CONFIDENCE

SCULPT, SHADE AND SHIMMER

CREATE THE FACE YOU WANT TO SHOW THE WORLD!

not GOOD

enough

15

The X Factor

Whatever the X factor is, I don't think I've got it. I'd rather crawl under a stone and hide than stand up and perform solo in front of Ked, Camille, my band mates and assorted others, but it seems I have no choice. Ritual humiliation is firmly on the schedule.

'It's just a bit of fun,' Ked explains over dinner. 'A bonding exercise. It'll help Camille, Mike and me to get to know you better, see what makes you tick. I want each of you to introduce yourselves – tell me a bit about what drives you, what matters to you. Then do a short solo turn that means something to you – Mike can sort you a soundtrack. There'll be no marking, no competition – I just want to find out more about you as individuals. Give it all you've got!'

All I've got is a gut full of fear.

'I don't have a single idea,' I whisper to Matt, picking listlessly at a plate of Mrs B's pasta bake. 'What are you going to do?'

'Me? Nothing!' Matt says cheerfully. 'I'm not in the band, remember! I plan to blend into the background and take notes on the rest of you!'

'Not helpful,' I growl.

Matt shrugs. 'Just pick a song you like, something relevant,' he suggests. 'D'you have any favourites? Lady Gaga? Ariana Grande? Rihanna?'

I almost laugh. Matt's way off the mark when it comes to my musical taste, but there's no reason for him to know that I like sixties stuff. I know he's only trying to help.

'I really like that Skeeter Davis song,' I say. 'The one about the end of the world. I could maybe do that?'

'Cheerful,' Matt quips. 'I've never heard of Skeeter Davis or the song, but then you're more of a muso than I am. D'you know it well enough to sing?'

'I think so . . . it's one of my gran's favourites. She taught me to sing it. It's really sad!'

Matt steals a forkful of my pasta. 'Do you *want* to sing a sad song?' he questions. 'Some old thing your gran used to sing? Maybe pick something a bit more upbeat, modern?'

I'm determined, though. I run over to ask Mike for the backing music.

'Nice choice,' he says. 'Sucker for a sad song, me! I'll get that set up, no worries.'

No worries . . . if only.

In the end, the X Factor evening is fun – or it would be, if I wasn't scheduled to go last. My stomach is in knots as I watch the others perform, but I can't help smiling at their efforts – I can see this is a fun, informal ice-breaker, but still, I can't help feeling scared.

Marley gives himself such a hyped-up intro that the rest of us can't help laughing, and he chooses to sing an old Carpenters song called 'Superstar'. Marley is playing it for laughs . . . but, as always with him, there's a streak of ruthless determination in what he does and we all know it. His little brother Dylan is next, explaining that he just loves music – it's all he's good at, all he cares about. He plays a long drum solo, possibly of his own creation, and it's brilliant.

Lexie says that songwriting has given her a way to express some of the difficult stuff inside her. She says she's a rescuer, but that the Lost & Found has actually rescued her . . . I can't help wishing I felt that way. Mike puts on the backing track of 'Library Song', because she says that's the one that started it all. She sings backing vocals and plays tambourine, and it's fantastic . . . I think Lexie is actually the heart of the band. And if she's the heart, Sami has to be the soul – his introduction is a short, simple thank-you to the band for being a lifeline, a lifesaver. He plays a gentle flute solo that makes me want to cry – it's so beautiful.

Bex goes next. If I had to pick a role for her within the band it'd be the conscience – Bex challenges Marley on his wilder flights of fancy, tells it like it is. She talks about having a rough start in life – she's in foster care, so I'm guessing there's something sad in her past – but claims that nothing will stop her getting to the top in whichever career she picks. 'Right now, I'd like it to be music,' she says. 'But when I retire from the band, I'll be a lawyer or an author, maybe . . .'

Mike puts on a Green Day backing track for her, and she plays an earth-shaking bass guitar solo.

Lee and George both reckon they hadn't found a real purpose in life until they joined the Lost & Found; Lee does a ska-style trumpet mash-up with some fancy dance steps, and George does a jazzy cello solo. When Happi steps up for her turn, she talks about her strict, religious parents and her dream of being a mathematician . . . as long as she can fit it in with being in the band! She plays a haunting classical violin solo.

'You'll leave those guys standing,' Matt says as Happi leaves the stage and Mike starts setting up for the next act. 'No contest!'

'It's not about that,' I argue. 'It's just a bit of fun . . .'

Matt shakes his head, as if he knows better than me. 'You should make an effort, maybe lose that jumper, let them see your figure . . .'

A little ache of hurt joins the panic in my chest. Nobody else has changed for this – we're all in jeans and jumpers and hoodies, the mismatched, casual clothes we've worn all day. I'd thought I looked good – apparently not.

'It's not a performance,' I whisper to Matt.

'Everything's a performance,' he replies, and I sigh because he has no idea just how true that is.

Romy is on stage now. I know how shy she is – I've tried to help her with her self-esteem . . . that's how we first bonded and became friends. Tonight she seems completely at ease as she tells everyone about her difficult home life and how everything has to revolve around looking after her mum. The band has opened new doors, given her a glimpse of a future she'd almost stopped hoping for. Romy plays her violin fiddle-style and sings an Irish ballad, and I'm so proud of my best friend I could hug her.

Jake is the last to take a turn.

'Why is he even in this?' Matt whispers. 'It's pointless!'

'He's doing it because he wants to,' I say.

Jake says he loves the band along with everyone in it, and is glad we treat him as part of it even though he can barely play the triangle. His life has been chaotic at times, he says, but things are better now and a lot of that is down to the Lost & Found. Jake's set up an amazing light show with one of the Lost & Found's tracks for backing, and I want to get lost in it but I can't, because it's my turn next and I am actually shaking with fear.

147

'Over to you, Sasha!' Jake says as the lights fade away. 'We saved the best till last!'

Matt whispers. 'Break a leg!'

I think I might. My legs are shaking as I stand and walk over to the stage. They feel so weak it seems impossible they will hold me up. I don't understand why my stage fright gets worse and worse, when my friends – even the shy ones – seem to be able to handle their moment in the spotlight. Perhaps it's fear of blanking out in front of everyone that makes my stomach churn? Standing here alone is even worse than when the band is behind me.

'So . . . Sasha?' Ked prompts, smiling.

My mouth feels dry as sawdust, the words I want to say tangled together in my head.

'I . . . never wanted to be a singer,' I begin, and I see Ked's frown and Marley's glare and know I've started this whole thing off on the wrong foot, veered way off course before I've even begun. 'I mean, I did – I used to pretend I was in a band when I was little, but I never actually planned for it to happen. What I mean is . . . I auditioned to play uke, and I'm quite good at keyboards but not as good as Soumia was . . . our first keyboard player. But Marley must have heard me singing somewhere along the line, because he asked me to audition for vocals, and here I am. Lead singer of a band!'

Ked and Camille are listening intently. My band mates look a little confused, unsure where I'm going with this. That's not surprising. I have no idea myself.

'What I'm trying to say is . . . I was always more of a background person, but now I'm here, fronting a band full of people who are probably – definitely – the best friends I've ever had. It's not always easy for me. Sometimes I think I'm just not good enough . . .'

I realize too late that I'm still wearing the blue jumper. A trickle of sweat slides down my neck and between my shoulder blades. I wish I could stop talking, stop digging a hole for myself. Somehow, away from Millford, the confident mask is slipping, revealing little glimpses of the way I really feel. This was not meant to happen.

I want to rewind, erase, put the anxious words back in their box and slam the lid tightly, but I can't. The words are out there now.

I take a deep breath and conjure a smile out of nowhere, the brightest, most dazzling smile I can find. I see Romy,

Lexie, Sami, Happi, Bex and Jake looking back at me, smiling, worried, willing me on. I see Matt, stupidly handsome, raising his camera to capture the smile, and Ked and Camille and the other adults watching me.

'You'll never know what the Lost & Found means to me,' I plough on. 'I can't believe how lucky I am to be a part of it! I've chosen to sing a sad song because it's one I've known since I was little, and it's beautiful, and because the Lost & Found are all about heartfelt, emotional music. It's an old sixties track by Skeeter Davis, and it's called "The End of the World".'

And suddenly it feels like the end of the world for real. I'm standing in the middle of the performance space and everyone is looking at me, and for a moment I have no idea why. In the background, a retro backing track is playing, and I remember that it's a track I'm supposed to be singing.

'Sasha?' Camille is saying. 'Is everything OK?'

'I don't know . . . I . . .'

'Start again?' Mike is asking, as the backing track fades into silence.

My cheeks are burning and every bit of me is shaking. It's not just myself I've let down, it's everyone, and the shame is heavy on my shoulders like the weight of the world.

If this is the X Factor, I'm out.

'I can't do this,' I whisper, and I turn and run.

Mum, I've tried calling but there's no answer on the house phone and your mobile's going straight to voicemail. Maybe you're out of battery or something? Feeling homesick. Can you give me a call back when you get this? Sash xx

Mum? Please? xx

16

Search Party

Where do you run when you're in a strange place far from home? I slip out through the back door into the darkness. I head away from the house and across the grass and over towards the copse of trees where Matt and I had breakfast earlier.

That feels like a million years ago.

Slumping down beneath a tree, I lean my head back against the rough bark, close my eyes and wish it would all go away.

My invisibility superpower only seems to work when it feels like it.

It takes a while for the panic and shame to subside, a while for the self-pity to kick in. If zone-out moments are caused by stress, I should be able to stop them by trying not to get wound up. The trouble is there's so much on my mind – fear of messing up, fear of being ill, of letting down the band. The worry that I'm getting into something I'm not quite sure about with Matt. And underneath, the crippling fear that things are going wrong again with Mum and Dad.

I hate feeling so helpless. Maybe Camille can help me to ditch the stage fright, ease the anxiety? Maybe Sheddie's yoga would help? And maybe when I get home I will find the courage to tell Mum and Dad what's going on with me – and ask them to tell me what's happening with them.

Maybe.

I'm shivering, chilled to the bone by the time I hear voices and spot a couple of moving torch beams coming closer in the darkness. My friends . . . what do I say to them? I rake the sleeve of my fluffy jumper across my eyes, but my breathing's still ragged and I'm way too embarrassed to talk to anyone.

I stay very still, hug my knees and press my face against the strands of ivy.

'Sasha? Sasha!' Romy's voice cuts through the velvet dark and my friends emerge from the gloom, picking their way through the undergrowth towards me.

My hiding skills are clearly not as good as they used to be.

'She's here!' Matt yells, bounding up to me and perching on a flat rock at my side. 'Sasha! Are you OK?'

'What's going on?' Bex demands, close behind him. 'What's up, Sash?'

'You can tell us,' Lexie promises.

'We can help,' Happi adds.

Jake doesn't say anything, just looks at me sadly. He's not going to tell anyone my secret, and for that I am glad.

'Was it . . . stage fright?' Romy asks gently. 'Because we've all been there. It was kind of odd being in the spotlight without the rest of the band.'

'I didn't like it,' Happi chips in. 'I pretended it was a science fair presentation, bluffed my way through.'

'Nobody cares,' Bex says with a shrug. 'Forget it, Sash. It was just a get-to-know-you exercise, nothing important.'

'Maybe,' I say.

But I know that I've given Ked, Camille and Mike the worst possible impression. They probably think I'm careless, cowardly and useless under pressure, with a tendency to run away when the going gets tough.

'Are you sure you're OK?' Lexie asks. 'I mean, you looked a bit lost for a minute back there. I thought you were going to faint . . .'

'Maybe it's a bug?' Matt suggests. 'Are you feeling ill?'

'Not really,' I tell him. 'Maybe. It's hard to explain.'

'We're happy to listen,' Romy says.

I sigh. 'I know,' I say. 'You're lovely, all of you. But I can't really explain . . . and I really, really wish it hadn't happened. Ked must be wondering what he's let himself in for, mentoring a band with a lead singer who wimps out at the slightest thing. As for Marley – he'll be raging. He'll never forgive me!'

Bex rolls her eyes. 'Ked won't care as long as you deliver the goods in the studio,' she declares. 'And Marley will get over it, trust me. He needs you – we all do, Sasha. Seriously . . . forget what happened. There's not one of us here who hasn't messed up big style at some point!'

156

'C'mon, come back up to the house,' Lexie says.

'In a bit,' I promise. 'I suppose . . . my pride's taken a knock, that's all. I just need a bit of time to get my head straight . . .'

'You want us to go?' Romy asks, frowning.

'I just . . . need a few minutes. I'm OK, honest!'

'I'll stay with her,' Matt states, throwing an arm across my shoulder. 'I'll bring her back. No worries.'

So the others head back to the house, and I'm left with Matt. I am not as thrilled about this as you might think, because over the last day or so I've had a few insights into Matt's character and I'm not sure he's quite as perfect as I first thought. Then again, I'm not exactly in a position to judge.

'Bit cold out here,' he says now, brushing twigs and leaves from his jeans and boots. 'No worries, though. I'll look after you!'

I force a smile, but the weight of Matt's arm is heavy on my shoulders. It doesn't feel comforting, warming or even romantic. It just feels like an extra burden.

Tears sting my eyes. What's wrong with me? The boy half the girls in my year group are crushing on is sitting

beside me in the dark, his arm round me, and still I'm not happy.

'You said you thought that Marley would be angry,' Matt is saying. 'Do you think so? Do the two of you not get along?'

'We get along fine,' I tell him, weary now. 'I just feel stupid, that's all. Embarrassed.'

'Could happen to anyone,' Matt says, but nobody else has messed up this way – panicked, blanked out, gone to pieces. Nobody but me.

'Do you think Marley's pushing you too hard?' Matt persists. 'He's very much the driving force behind the band, isn't he? Do you feel he's expecting too much? Being heavy-handed?'

I frown and shift slightly, shrugging off Matt's embrace. I feel all kinds of uncomfortable. I don't want to be hugged, although he's not exactly being huggy; it's more like he's acting a part, staking a claim. I can't help thinking he's fishing for dirt on the band, looking for an angle to write something dramatic.

He wouldn't do that, though, surely?

I bite my lip. I'd like to trust Matt, but I can't.

I'm not sure I even like him.

'What is it, Sash?' he wheedles, nudging me playfully. 'I know Marley can be a bit of a slave driver. Have the two of you had a row? A disagreement? You can tell me.'

The arm is back, round my waist this time, pulling me close.

'You and me, Sasha, we're a great team,' Matt is saying. 'You're sensitive, I get that, but I'll look out for you . . . stick up for you. I don't think you even know how gorgeous you really are.'

This is something I've been imagining for weeks. The coolest boy in Year Eleven falling for me, telling me I'm gorgeous . . . my heart is racing, but not in a good way. I feel out of my depth, alarmed, even slightly scared.

What is it with me and my dreams? The minute they start to come true, they turn to dust in my hands.

Matt lunges at my face, his mouth on mine, too warm, too wet, tasting of the tuna pasta we had for tea. He's pushing me back against the tree trunk, one hand buried in my hair, the other tugging at my jumper. I feel like I might suffocate, or possibly scream.

This is my first kiss, and it's nothing like the movies say it is. It's rough and clumsy and frightening.

My hands curl into fists, pushing against his chest, shoving him away from me.

'*No!*' I yell, and I'm surprised at the force of the push, the volume of the yell.

Matt seems surprised too. I watch the shock on his face turn slowly to disdain.

'Look . . . I'm not ready for anything like this,' I say, and my voice is shaking. 'I like you . . . but as a friend, y'know?'

'A friend?' he echoes, his mouth curled into a sneer. 'What are you, five years old?'

'Matt, please!'

'Forget it,' he says, a little stiffly. 'Maybe I was getting mixed messages, Sasha, but I don't think you actually know what you want. I was trying to be a friend. I thought maybe you could use one, but it looks like I was wrong. Sorry I bothered!'

He looks angry, and I am pretty sure he won't be calling for me tomorrow to go for a breakfast picnic. Way to go, Sasha.

Matt strides away into the darkness and I am left shaking, unsure whether to laugh or cry. Did I really have a crush

on this boy? He's mad at me because I haven't dished any dirt on the band to feed his craving for some kind of shock-horror scoop, and because I didn't like being pawed and slobbered on. What a creep!

The first tear is sliding soundlessly down my cheek when I hear the sound of twigs cracking, leaves crunching. Looking up, I see the silhouette of someone approaching – a boy.

'Matt, just leave me alone!' I snap, exasperated.

The figure halts, hands held high in a gesture of surrender.

'Not Matt – Jake,' a familiar voice says. 'It's OK. I get the message . . . I was just checking you were OK.'

My breath huffs out with relief.

'Jake . . . sorry! I thought it was Matt. He just wouldn't leave me be!'

Jake steps into a little pool of moonlight, keeping his distance, huddled in his jacket. As usual, his hair is sticking up in three or four different directions.

'I saw him marching back up to the house,' he says. 'He looked pretty hacked off. I won't stay, I just . . . dunno, I wanted to make sure you were OK. I worry about you.'

'Don't,' I tell him. 'I'm fine. And . . . well, you don't have to go, not unless you want to. Matt was bugging me, that's all.'

Jake sits down beside me, cross-legged in the fallen leaves. He hands me a clean tissue from his pocket and I dry my eyes, blow my nose. I cringe to think what I must look like . . . panda eyes, smeary eyeshadow, pink nose. Right now, I don't even care.

'Did he do something to upset you?' Jake asks quietly. 'If he did . . .'

'It doesn't matter,' I say, although it does, of course. Every time I think of my first kiss I'll remember horrible Matt Brennan trying to stick his tongue in my mouth. Yuck.

'I just didn't want to talk to him, that's all,' I say to Jake. 'He's not the person I thought he was.'

'Arrogant, selfish, ruthlessly ambitious,' Jake quips. 'What's not to like?'

I laugh, in spite of myself. 'You had him sussed from the start, didn't you?' I say. 'Sadly, I didn't. I wish he wasn't here with us . . . I don't think I trust him.'

'I definitely don't,' he replies. 'But he's here now, so we'd better get used to it.'

'I guess . . .'

There's a silence, and I shiver, hugging myself against the cold. Jake shrugs off his jacket and hands it to me, and I don't even try to argue. I take it and pull it round my shoulders.

'Thank you,' I whisper. 'Next time I go running off in a strop I'll pick better weather.'

'Yeah, good plan,' Jake says. 'Last time I ran away, I timed it for the summer holidays. Wall-to-wall sunshine . . .'

I blink. 'You're joking, right?'

'Sort of,' he says with a grin. 'It rained some of the time. I did run away, though. I'll tell you about it sometime. So . . . what happened back there? You blanked out again?'

I can feel my cheeks burning. 'Don't tell anybody! Please!'

He rolls his eyes. 'I won't,' he tells me. 'I'd have done that already if I was going to, wouldn't I? You know what I think, Sasha. You can't just pretend this isn't happening.'

'I can,' I argue. 'At least – I'm trying!'

'Is it working?'

'Not exactly!'

The two of us huddle side by side beneath the trees. Above us, through the branches, the sky is a dark inky blue pierced with a scattering of stars, the moon a sliver of cool silver-white.

Jake is a much easier person to be with than Matt. He doesn't ask ridiculous questions or paw me as if he owns me. He just sits quietly, not hassling, not judging. A silence settles around us, peaceful, calm. Inside the silence, I can feel my anxiety peeling away.

'Look!'

I follow Jake's glance, gazing across the darkened hollow of grass. My eyes focus on the silhouette of a fox moving quickly, tail flicking behind. The breath catches in my throat and a surge of pure joy rises up inside me.

The world is more than thinking you have a crush on a boy, then freaking out when he tries to get up close and personal. It's more than some get-to-know-you game, more than the band, more than the tasks set out for us this week. The Lost & Found are just a tiny cog in the machinery of it all, and I am just one small part of that cog.

Maybe I'm not perfect. Maybe I'm too anxious to perform on stage and maybe there is something going on that makes me blank out every now and then.

Whatever that old sixties song says, maybe it's not the end of the world.

Sorry, Mum. Ignore those last few messages. Was having a drama queen moment and feeling homesick and sorry for myself. I'm OK – better than OK, actually. Love you. Give Dad a hug from me. I'll ring you in the morning. So much to tell you! Sash xx

17

The Midnight Meeting

When we get back to Fox Hollow Hall, we're ambushed by the others and dragged into the living room for a council of war.

The adults have tactfully disappeared, but the whole band is here, plus Matt with his camera and his slightly sneering smile. It's a calculating smile – how come I've never noticed that before?

'Better now?' he asks coldly. 'Chatted it all through with Jake, have you?'

'No, I –'

'Whatever,' he snaps. 'No worries.'

I think I have made an enemy.

My friends are huddled round the wood burner, draped across the sofas, spread across floor cushions. Even Mary Shelley the tortoise is here, ploughing her way through a little pile of curly kale leaves and looking up occasionally to send me a sympathetic glance. At least she won't judge me – I hope.

Jake and I sit side by side, cross-legged on a sheepskin rug. Lexie and Happi come in with trays laden with mugs of hot chocolate and chocolate-chip cookies, and I take one of each to warm up a little and sweeten the blow of what's to come.

I can't read Marley's expression, but he can't be pleased at my diva moment, I know. I've let him down, let the band down . . . I understand that without anyone having to spell it out.

'It's pretty intense, isn't it?' Marley begins, sipping his hot chocolate. 'This mentoring thing. A whole different ball game from our practice sessions at home. Maybe the X Factor spoof felt a bit . . . well, exposing for some of you. We're all out of our comfort zone, right?'

'Right,' the others chorus.

'I'm so sorry. I just . . . I'm not quite sure what happened there!' The words burst out of me, a jumble of regret and shame. 'I feel awful!'

Marley sighs. 'I know,' he says. 'And you shouldn't, Sasha. It was just a blip – I know that. We all have those stage-fright moments sometimes. Who cares if you can't do a neat little speech to order? You're a singer, not an actress! You just lost your mojo there for a moment.'

Marley is defending me . . . That's not what I expected.

'I know you feel bad,' he ploughs on. 'Look, I want you to put what happened right out of your mind. This is no time to let yourself fall apart . . . we all have to work harder than we ever have before to make the most of this week. I want everyone at yoga, everyone at studio practice and the workshops. It doesn't matter whether you think it'll help you or not – do it anyway, yeah?'

'Yeah . . . sure . . .' I mumble. 'I am really sorry . . .'

'Hey,' Marley says kindly. 'Sasha, nobody here would ever doubt your commitment to the Lost & Found, least of all me. You're our lead singer. That might feel like a lot of pressure, but we have your back!'

I'm grinning, weak with relief. 'I won't let you down,' I promise. 'I lost the plot, but it won't happen again . . .'

I trail away into silence, because, in spite of my best efforts, it probably will happen again. My promises are worth nothing. Beside me, Jake gazes politely down into his hot chocolate, silent.

I hope he understands how much I want a fresh chance. I think he does.

Matt, by contrast, looks sceptical, like he can see inside my head and suss out the wishful thinking. He wouldn't call it that, of course – he'd call it a lie.

Mary Shelley ambles over on some secret mission, and I scoop her up on to my knees, stroking her. What I wouldn't give right now to be a tortoise – there'd be no daily struggle to be something I'm not, to be perfect, confident, a star in the making. And I'd have my own ready-made hiding place whenever I wanted it.

'I know you won't let us down,' Marley is saying. 'Besides, any one of us can mess up. Remember the night before our first big gig, the festival in the park when I got into a fight and almost wrecked everything? Who rescued me? You lot did, and Sasha managed to camouflage the cuts and bruises so I didn't look like roadkill. We stuck together and we'll do the same now. I'll talk to Ked and Camille about helping you to work on stage fright and nerves.'

I nod, ashamed to be singled out for special help, but grateful too. If there's a way to sort this thing, I'll try it, no question.

'If you're trying hard now, I want you all to try harder still tomorrow,' Marley concludes. 'The stronger we are as a team, the better the Lost & Found will be. We're in this together, and we have to stay solid. All for one . . .'

'And one for all!' a couple of the boys chime, doing their best Three Musketeers impression. Matt rolls his eyes, unimpressed, and I wonder why I haven't noticed his mean streak before. Better late than never, I guess.

There are lots of hugs and kind words as we clear up and head for our rooms, and I pass Mary Shelley over to Lexie with a sigh. Though Jake only squeezes my hand as he heads after the other boys, that touch means more than any of the others.

I have another chance, a chance not to mess up, I remind myself as I snuggle beneath the duvet and drift towards sleep. Maybe this time I won't blow it.

I still sleep badly. Every time I check my phone, time seems to be passing more slowly, but at last the thin light of dawn pokes through the curtains and I creep to the bathroom, hoping a shower will revive me. It works . . . for a little while, at least.

Marley's pep talk has pulled us all together, because everyone – except Matt – turns out for Sheddie's yoga class. It's not bad. I like the feeling that we're all in this together . . . Lexie, Jake and Happi move easily through the poses. Bex, Marley, Dylan and Lee take it too seriously, glancing around to see if they're getting it right. George, Romy and Sami look slightly lost but push on all the same. None of us are experts here. We're all beginners, all trying something new and doing our best.

The flowing, gentle movements somehow switch off the crazy scribble of anxiety in my head, and I'm calm, content, living in the moment – stretching tall, breathing deeply and letting go of every little shred of tension and worry during the relaxation at the end of the session. I don't zone out once.

Afterwards, sitting cross-legged on my yoga mat on the dew-damp grass, I feel calmer than I have for ages. Maybe yoga is something I could do back home to keep the stress at bay.

'Who knew yoga would be cool?' I say to Romy. 'Fancy finding a class back home in Millford?'

'You bet!' she says. 'OK . . . I'm grabbing the first shower. See you in a bit!' She heads back to the house with the others, but I linger a while, smiling because I feel I'm taking control, finding new ways to try to sort my problems. It feels good.

Jake comes to a halt beside me and we pause for a while, watching the ice-cream colours of the sky, dramatic behind the bare-branched trees. The day ahead seems filled with possibilities.

'Starshine Festival soon,' he reminds me. 'Should be fun!'

'It should – just what I need.'

No voice coaching, no X Factor, no pressure . . . and right now just me and Jake, quietly drinking in the magic of Fox Hollow Hall.

Sometimes, in little moments like this, I really am happy.

'Sasha! Jake! There you are!' Camille's voice rings out, breaking the spell. 'Don't forget the minibus is leaving at nine!'

'Don't want to be late!' Jake grins, and we jump up and head inside. The others are all changed and ready and eating breakfast, fizzing with anticipation. Romy is wearing the fifties dress she borrowed from me, sashaying round the kitchen with a slice of toast and marmalade.

I head upstairs to change out of my yoga stuff. The bedrooms are empty, the connecting door open between them from when we scrambled to get ready for yoga earlier. Clothes are strewn across the beds and Mary Shelley is drifting across the scrubbed-pine floorboards in search of inspiration. I know the feeling.

'You're on your own today,' I tell her, going to find the tortoise food stash and adding a few tiny slivers of red pepper to her dish.

I make a quick call home to say I'm OK, but Mum sounds as if she's trying too hard to reassure me that everything's fine. I can't help feeling something's off.

Pushing the thought away, I put together an outfit for the festival. Little print dress, rust-coloured tights and cardie, lace-up boots and beret . . . I look good, good enough to be the singer in an up-and-coming band, good enough to show Matt Brennan that I won't be pining for him any time soon.

I take five minutes to do my make-up, blending brown and gold eyeshadow and adding my trademark cat's eye flick. A swipe of clear lip gloss and I'm good to go.

'What d'you think, Mary Shelley?' I ask, doing a little twirl.

I'm sure I see a glint of approval in her eyes, and on impulse I snap a few pictures of her at my feet, nestled in my favourite mustard-coloured scarf. I'll edit and upload it to my Instagram feed later.

I run downstairs to grab a croissant and find the kitchen empty except for Mrs B clearing tables. As she adds an empty juice glass to the tower of plates she's carrying, a handful of dirty cutlery slips off and clatters to the floor.

'Oh dear! I don't know what's wrong with me today!'

I duck down to help gather them up.

'Thank you,' she says with a sigh. 'I'm not feeling too well. I've a splitting headache, but at least I get the rest of the day off with you lot at the festival. You'd better hurry – Mike brought the minibus round a while ago!'

Jake's grinning face peeps round the kitchen door.

'Been looking for you everywhere,' he says. 'We're all ready to go! C'mon!'

He grabs my hand and pulls me out towards the waiting minibus.

SashaSometimes

♡ ◯ ◁   ⊓

227 likes

SashaSometimes Latest member of the behind-the-scenes crew for the Lost & Found . . . meet Mary Shelley #ShellShocked #Lost&Found #BandLife

Tilly08 So cute!

littlejen Is that your tortoise?

SaraLou Love the name, very clever!

Kezsez07 My friend's got a tortoise!

Brownie Did she write Frankenstein? Impressive!

Lil_Chels Are you working with Ked Wilder this week?

MattBFotos Boring

JBSings Shut up @MattBFotos nobody asked your opinion!

18

Wonderland

Starshine is the coolest thing I've ever seen. Ked has arranged VIP passes for the festival, so we don't have to queue. We're given maps of the arena village – a huge, purpose-built complex of linked exhibition halls, lecture theatres and gallery spaces – and then set loose until our lunch meeting at one.

'Soak up the atmosphere, have fun, get inspired!' Ked tells us. 'I want you to enjoy the music, try out new things, learn all you can and feel the magic – because if all goes to plan, you'll be playing here next year. OK – see you in Meeting Room Three at one o'clock. Go!'

The arena village looks amazing – the high ceilings are pinned with white billowing fabric, lit up with a kaleidoscope of changing colours. The stalls and spaces are like stage sets from some future fantasy world, and four of the main exits lead into huge festival tents, already mobbed and each with its own schedule of bands and performers. We're wide-eyed, smiling so hard it hurts, amazed at this glimpse of a world we could one day be part of.

'Wow,' Jake says into my ear. 'Where do we even start?'

There are gigs all day by performers ranging from new talent to big names. There are talks, workshops, interviews and hundreds of stalls offering everything from clothes, CDs and vinyl to musical instruments and tech gear. One whole hall is devoted to showcasing music industry freelancers – lighting experts and sound specialists, stylists, photographers, film-makers, even indie TV and radio channels, and Radio 1 is broadcasting live from the venue all day.

Marley tries to make a plan, but we all want to do different things, and the place is so huge and so busy it's impossible to explore as a group. Almost at once, Marley, Dylan, Lee and Bex get sidetracked watching the Chaotic Umbrellas, a screeching punk band dressed in what looks like ragged bandages. Mandy, Jon and Sheddie head off to find coffee, while George, Sami and Happi sign up for a talk about degree courses in music. Jake grabs the last place in a stage-lighting workshop, flashing me a wave as he files into the studio.

Lexie, Romy and I are left alone.

'Let's choose one thing each,' I suggest. 'That way we get to do more!'

'I want to road-test an electric violin,' Romy says at once.

'I want to watch the Smile Sandwich gig over in the New Talent tent at half eleven,' Lexie adds.

'I'd like to check out the industry showcase area,' I decide. 'Look at the film-makers and stylists and stuff. Violin first?'

Romy causes a stir at the violin stall by playing a sizzling piece from our song 'Setting Sun' on a top-of-the-range electric violin that costs almost as much as my mum earns in a year, but she decides electric is not for her. We linger in the acoustic tent and watch Lexie's pick, a cute folky duo . . . they're fresh and cool and we all love their set. Finally, we head for the industry area.

It's fascinating – there are so many businesses linked to the music world that could help us to showcase our skills.

Some offer lighting effects or promo videos, some will print your band name on a T-shirt or a bag, some will style and photograph you and make you look like you belong on the cover of *Vogue*.

'What happened to Matt?' Lexie asks. 'So much for being our official photographer and documenting our every move!'

'Probably sulking somewhere,' I say. 'My fault. We kind of fell out last night – I think he's avoiding me.'

'His pride's taken a dent,' Romy comments. 'He's probably used to girls falling at his feet!'

'I can't work him out,' Lexie adds. 'I know Marley thinks he'll be useful to the band, though.'

'I thought he was great,' I admit. 'But maybe it wasn't really Matt I fell for, just an imaginary version of him. The real Matt's not quite as cool as I thought.'

I think of last night's clumsy struggle of a kiss, and know I've had a lucky escape.

'Boys,' Romy sighs. 'They're a complete mystery to me!'

Lexie pulls me towards a stall where a make-up artist is transforming a man from the crowd into a kind of zombie in an amazing special-effects demo. We watch, loving it,

then move on to the next space where the make-up is less gruesome and punters are giving each other a series of DIY fantasy makeovers. The workbenches are a treasure trove of vivid colours begging to be explored.

My heart races just looking at it, and when the super-cool young woman behind the counter gestures towards one of the work stations, we jump at the chance. 'Create any look you want,' she tells us. 'The wilder, the better!'

Surprisingly, Romy volunteers to be guinea pig. 'Make me look cool,' she requests, trying to sound brave. 'Make me look like I belong in a band!'

'Your wish is my command,' I tease. 'This'll make George sit up and take notice!'

'What if he laughs at me?' Romy panics.

'Not a chance!'

I know this is outside her comfort zone, so I keep Romy chatting as Lexie wraps the nylon cape round her shoulders, covering up the bright fifties frock. I sense her starting to relax, leaning back in the chair, eyes drifting shut as I sponge on the primer and base. I shade her cheekbones, add some barely there highlighter and dust with translucent powder. Picking out a palette of coppery browns and golds for Romy's eyes, I sweep eyeliner under her lashes, add two coats of mascara and finish with gold glitter dabbed across her cheekbones.

'Hair up?' Lexie suggests. 'So we can actually see what you've done?' Romy spends her days hiding behind her hair, which is mousy brown and straight with a heavy fringe.

'Aww no,' she protests, but still manages to find a comb and a handful of mini hairbands in her bag. The woman from the counter appears with cans of mousse and hairspray, and when I look up I see a little knot of onlookers watching Romy's transformation. No pressure then. I scoosh in some mousse and go mad with backcombing to get a bit of volume, then comb the fringe up and back into the rest of her hair to form five twisty little buns. A spritz of lacquer and Romy is done.

My friend looks gorgeous – without the fringe you can see her big brown eyes and pretty heart-shaped face. Romy blinks at her reflection as if she can't quite believe it.

'What did you do?' she asks, astonished. 'I look . . . so different! This'd be a great stage look!'

'It really would,' Lexie agrees. 'Sash, can you do me too?'

She slips into the chair. This time I work more confidently, picking blues and silvers to complement Lexie's colouring. I brush some of the jewel-bright eyeshadow through Lexie's brows, dust glitter across her cheekbones and wonder if I can risk turquoise lips.

The woman from the counter drifts up behind me. 'You have a talent for this,' she tells me. 'Seriously, you do! Come back later this afternoon and I'll make you up. I'd do it now, but I have a lunch meeting . . .'

I look at my phone, panicked. 'Oh no – so do we! At Meeting Room Three . . .'

The woman starts to laugh. 'One o'clock, with Ked Wilder?' she guesses. 'I should have known! You three must be from the Lost & Found, right? I'm Ria and this is Fitz – we're your lunch dates!'

Fitz turns out to be a slightly camp hipster dressed in a vintage waistcoat and cravat, his trousers rolled up to reveal brown vintage brogues and bare ankles. A camera hangs round his neck. He's fussing a little, briefing a couple of young assistants who'll be holding the fort for a while before turning to us with a big grin.

'Mustn't be late,' he says, whisking us away into the crush.

'Ked's asked us to work with you on developing a stage image,' Ria explains as we weave through the crowd. 'Though I'm not so sure you need our help!'

'Perhaps just a little . . .' Fitz says tactfully.

We reach the meeting room dead on time, but Ked and the others are already there – even Matt. A long table has been set with a tapas-style buffet. There are platters of empanadas and sliced tortilla, roasted figs with honey and goat's cheese, steaming paella and even a mountain of warm churros with glossy chocolate sauce . . . it looks amazing.

'OK,' Ked is saying. 'I hope you've had fun so far. Time for lunch now and a couple of meetings. First of all, meet Ria and Fitz – they're going to create your new stage look. They'll be coming to Fox Hollow Hall next week to transform you, but I thought it made sense if they could meet you now, get a sense of who you are.'

'Ked sent over a couple of film clips of the Lost & Found in action,' Ria tells us. 'We have some ideas already, but we want to be sure we're on the right track. Fitz wants to take some quick portraits so we can plan colours.'

'All very painless,' Fitz promises. 'Pretend I'm not here.' He holds up his camera, snaps a picture of Marley and winks.

185

'I thought I was the photographer,' Matt mutters. 'Shouldn't I be doing the portraits?'

Ked frowns. 'You're doing a formal band shoot after the styling next week,' he tells Matt. 'I think we'll let the professionals do what they need to do, OK?'

'Yes, of course,' Matt says, backtracking rapidly. 'I didn't mean to be pushy – I'm just keen to be useful. Sorry!'

I don't think Ked is fooled, but Fitz ignores the exchange and the rest of us take plates and help ourselves to the tapas, swapping stories about what we've been doing.

'How was the lighting workshop?' I ask Jake with a grin. 'Illuminating?'

'Funny,' he says. 'It was cool – definitely gave me a few *bright* ideas. What did you do?'

'I made my friends look like cute, cool aliens,' I quip, watching as Romy poses for her photo, newly confident in her glitter and fifties dress. It gives me a kick to know that a few strokes of make-up can boost her confidence so much.

'We need to use the glitter theme in your new look,' Ria tells me. 'We were thinking of a sixties theme, and this space-style take on it would fit really well. I meant what I said – you have a talent for this. Anyone can learn to contour, but creativity and an instinctive eye for colour and drama is something you can't teach. Let me know if you ever get tired of being lead singer!'

I laugh. 'I will! I really do love make-up. It's awesome to meet someone who knows what an art form it can be. I can't wait to see what you have in store for us next week!'

'Ah, Sasha,' Ked says, gliding up beside me. 'It's great to see you looking so fired up! I have a little interview in the pipeline for you, Marley and Lexie. Radio 1 is broadcasting live from the festival and they'd like to meet you. It's nothing scary – they just want to hear how you feel about what it's like to be such a young band getting great reviews. They'll ask about this week in Devon, the mentoring thing, the new EP. And what you think of Starshine Festival, of course!'

Marley and Lexie are just behind him, their faces bright with excitement. 'Radio 1!' Marley breathes. 'Can't quite believe it!'

But my mouth feels dry as dust and there's a knot of panic in my gut. 'I don't know . . . I don't think I can do that!'

'Why not?' Ked frowns as if my words make no sense to him. 'It's just answering a few simple questions.'

187

'On live radio,' I add. 'Yes, I know. I can't do that, Ked – I'm really sorry!'

'C'mon, Sasha!' Marley argues. 'You're our lead singer! People want to hear from you!'

'It's not as scary as it sounds,' Lexie chips in.

But the waves of panic crashing through my body tell another story. 'I'm just not the right person for this,' I plead. 'I get so nervous and I can't think straight. How about Bex or Sami or Happi?'

I've messed up in style on live radio before – it's not something I want to repeat. Marley looks annoyed, but Ked nods his head slowly. 'You're sure?' he checks.

I look past Ked and catch Jake's eye. He nods softly, grinning and raking a hand through his tawny blond hair. He understands, I know.

'I'm sure.'

In the end, Sami steps in and the three of them do a brilliant interview that lasts way longer than planned and manages to cover the topics of refugee children, creativity, starting out in the music business and working with the legendary Ked Wilder. The rest of us watch and listen from the makeshift Green Room, and when it's over the DJ plays a rough-cut recording of our song 'Train of Thought'.

'Watch out for the Lost & Found,' he declares. 'They're going to be big – and you heard them here first!'

Marley's on too much of a high after that to remember to be mad at me and, besides, Ked's set up another meeting for us, this time with the OK Film team who are tasked with making a promo video for our first single. Like our chat with Ria and Fitz, this is pretty informal – we haven't chosen our debut single yet, so it's impossible to plan in detail. Ollie and Krish from OK outline their idea of filming us singing live as if at a big gig, and intercutting this with more informal shots of the band wandering around the grounds of Fox Hollow Hall.

'It's a great setting,' Ollie says. 'Crazy not to use it! Once you've settled on a song we'll tighten things up and see what else we need.'

'One thing's certain, mind,' Krish adds. 'You'll be the star, Sasha – lead singer and all that. You've got a great look, and we've seen the ideas Ria and Fitz have for styling. We'll get your face on all the music channels, the kids' pop shows, the music mags. You're going to be famous, girl!'

My smile freezes, slips sideways. I feel sick and shaky, full of dread.

'What if –' I begin, but Marley stops me mid-sentence.

'That sounds amazing,' he says to Krish. 'I can totally imagine it. We can't wait for Thursday, can we, guys?'

'No . . . can't wait,' I whisper. I can dodge out of doing a live radio interview, but avoiding the promo video? That's going to be impossible.

Later – much later – I've danced away the panic to the music of four amazing bands in the main stage tent, laughed so hard the tears roll down my cheeks and lost my new beret in the crowd. I've hugged my friends and told them I love them, scuffed my boots beyond repair, wrapped glow-sticks round my wrists and poured a paper cup of iced water over my head in an attempt to cool down. I have only zoned out two or three times all day, which is a bit of a record lately, and every time I came back to myself I found Jake beside me, his hand in mine, telling me I was OK.

By the time the fifth band begin their set, I'm exhausted. I want to watch them – they won one of the reality talent

shows a couple of years ago and have had a string of upbeat, poppy hits – but I'm wiped out and weary.

'Enough?' Jake asks, and when I nod he takes my hand and leads me out of the crush and back through the arena.

'Chill-out tent,' Jake says.

'Huh?'

I must have missed it earlier – the chill-out tent is a kind of wonderland, a beautiful space scattered with Indian rugs and cushions. Prayer flags and lanterns hang everywhere. The tent roof shimmers with a projected image of an indigo sky scattered with stars, and even the air smells sweet and spicy with incense. On the makeshift stage someone is playing a hypnotic-sounding instrument I've never seen or heard before, and Jake says it's a sitar. He fetches us fruit smoothies and we find a corner to flop down and rest, and even though I'm certain my make-up has smudged and my hair has gone frizzy, I can't remember being this happy for a very long time.

'An hour, then we'd best head out and find the minibus,' Jake says.

An hour. I could stay here forever, cross-legged on an Indian rug beside this boy I am starting to like as more than

191

a friend, this boy with hair that sticks up in every direction, with his chocolate-lime addiction and his quiet kindness and lopsided grin.

I could stay here forever, but if that's not possible I'll settle for however long we have.

SashaSometimes

211 likes

SashaSometimes Starshine Festival!
#DreamComeTrue #SoHappy #Lost&Found #BestBand
#BestFriends

MillfordGirl1 First like!

OllieK So jealous!

Sweet22 You're at Starshine! #LifeGoals

Jo_05 Were you playing?

Lil_Chels Heard you on the radio earlier!

littlejen VIP!!!

SaraLou Did you take the tortoise?

Musicismylife So happy for you!

19

Mask

It looks like Monday has been cancelled due to lack of interest. The minibus didn't get back until the early hours and there's no yoga because Sheddie's slept in. So have half my band mates, and there's no aroma of coffee and warm croissants in the kitchen when I go in search of breakfast. Instead, I find Camille hauling sliced bread from the freezer and ransacking the cupboards for marmalade and jam.

'Mrs B has flu,' she tells me. 'High fever, aching bones, can't get out of bed – we're on our own. It'll be DIY breakfast today . ... I'll see if I can defrost this bread!'

'No worries,' I tell her. 'We're not going to starve, are we?'

Camille laughs. 'No, definitely not!'

In the end, I run through my vocal exercises right there in the kitchen, and Camille shares her best tips for getting calm and centred before a performance. Her confidence is catching, and my spirits soar at the thought of taking control of the anxiety.

Lexie appears with Mary Shelley in her cardboard carrying case. 'I've been writing,' she says, dropping a notebook on to the zinc-topped table. 'Inspired by that collage from the other day – all those cut-outs from the beauty mags. Can't get it out of my head.'

I blink, secretly thrilled that one of my ideas might make song status.

Camille makes more toast as Bex, Romy, Happi and Jake drift down to join us, followed by Marley, Lee, George and Sami. I notice Camille tidying away a few wine glasses and empty bottles from the living room, which may explain why most of the adults are missing in action this morning.

Without Ked's guidance, our studio songwriting workshop starts slowly. Lexie lies on the floor, scrawling new lines, chopping things around, piecing words together jigsaw style, while Mary Shelley the tortoise rustles gently through the dozens of ideas and papers from Saturday spread across the floor. Bex picks up her bass and starts to play around with riffs and chords, while Romy and Happi put together a gentle violin melody. Sami picks up his flute and joins in.

'The song's about masks,' Lexie tells us. 'I have loads of ideas – maybe there are actually two songs here? I can't tell. Standing out and blending in, wanting to be seen and wanting to pass unnoticed . . .'

'Like a game of hide-and-seek,' I chip in, and Lexie nods, scribbling down my words.

'Sometimes just fitting in is all I actually want to do,' Happi says. 'I don't want to stand out. Not for the way I look, anyway!'

'We want to be seen for who we are,' Jake adds. 'Not what others want us to be. That's something we can't always live up to.'

Our eyes meet briefly and we exchange a grin. He has a way of tapping into the heart of things. I can't help wondering whether he's talking about me, or whether this is just the way we all feel.

'I hate being judged,' I find myself saying. 'When you're part of a band like the Lost & Found the judgements never stop. You're the lead singer, so you must be confident, flirty, brave . . . I'm not any of those things!'

'I think you're brave,' Jake says, so quietly that I'm not sure anyone else hears. I feel my cheeks flare with pink.

'People look at me and think I'm swotty and shy and boring,' Romy chips in. 'It makes me sad because I know there's so much more to me than that. I loved the glitter make-up you did for me yesterday, Sash – that felt like putting on a mask, but it also felt like freedom. It gave me the courage to be me!'

'Looked incredible,' George comments, then coughs and turns a startling shade of crimson that matches Romy's.

'It was great to see you so confident!' I tell her, trying not to smile. 'Why are people always so judgy? We stick labels on each other all the time. Then we have to live with those labels – and sometimes we try to live up to them too . . .'

I think of my Instagram feed, deliberately styled to show a perfect girl, loving life, having fun. It's a real work of

fiction – even I don't recognize the girl in the pictures. It's just another mask.

'I'm done with labels,' Romy states. 'I'm just me. Take it or leave it!'

'We'll take it,' Bex says, looking up from her bass. 'Be yourself, and never apologize for it – even if you're shaking in your shoes!'

'I'm shaking,' Dylan quips, sneaking in quietly, his hair still damp from the shower. Marley tells him to shut up, and Dylan pulls a face but does as he's told. We're all here now, and there's a sense that something cool is happening.

'You know who my role model is? Mary Shelley!' Lexie tells us, watching the little tortoise mooching around the studio. 'She's always chilled. She doesn't struggle with trying to be something she's not.'

'Be more Mary,' Jake says, and everyone laughs.

'Maybe,' I say. 'If Mary wants to shut the world out for a bit, she can withdraw into her shell any time she likes. I envy that. I've spent years wishing I could disappear, be invisible. I used to think it would be cool – a sort of freedom. But maybe it'd be scary too . . .'

I want to say more. I want to say that if you spend your whole life trying to be invisible, then maybe one day you will disappear for real. I want to tell Lexie and Happi and Romy about the black-hole moments, but it feels too big a thing to say, even with Jake here for moral support. I don't think I have the words, and I don't want to be the one to ruin this moment when we're all working together, sharing ideas, creating something new.

Lexie pulls together a song that feels so raw, so personal, I don't quite know how I'll be able to sing it. The finished lyrics are passed round, and Marley begins to shape a tune. When I look up, I notice that Ked has come in and is sitting on the windowsill beside Camille, watching, smiling.

We break for lunch an hour later than scheduled, with the mask song sounding great. Mandy, Jon and Sheddie have taken over the cooking, and we eat baked potatoes with cheese and beans, and lament the loss of Mrs B's cakes and puddings.

'We could just do our own?' Happi suggests, and moments later Romy, Jake and I are up and hunting for flour and butter and sugar while Happi Googles a foolproof recipe for chocolate brownies. We're a long way from *Bake Off* standard, but it's fun to beat the eggs and fold them into the butter and sugar, fun to whisk in cocoa powder and flour to make a glossy batter.

Lexie isn't baking – all through lunch she sits on the big window seat, nibbling absently at an apple as she scribbles in her notebook. She's so immersed in what she's doing that she's barely aware of Sami, who sits sketching at her feet, or Mary Shelley, who patrols around her, a small tortoise-shaped bodyguard. The rest of us give her space in case another song is forming.

There's a blob of chocolate cake mix on Jake's nose and a dusting of flour across his T-shirt. His tongue pokes out a little as he concentrates.

'We could pick some apples later and make a crumble for tomorrow,' he suggests. 'There are five or six apple trees behind the studio. Later?'

'OK,' I say, grinning.

'This week has been a blast so far,' he declares. 'It's just what we needed. Lexie's fizzing with ideas . . . the rest of us are learning loads . . . and yesterday at Starshine was epic.

Best of all, it turns out I'm a natural with a whisk. Who knew?'

'See if you're a natural with the washing up,' Romy scolds, chucking him a tea towel. 'And try not to flood the place, OK?'

By the time the brownies are out of the oven and cool enough to try, Lexie is leaning back, reading through her notes. Slowly a big smile spreads across her face.

'Another song?' I ask, offering her the first pick of the cakes. 'You were miles away back there . . . I guess inspiration hit.'

'It was what we were saying earlier about being seen,' Lexie says with a shrug. 'And wanting to disappear. I had an idea and I wanted to get it down . . . I've kind of gone off at a tangent, but I think it might be good. Maybe!'

Marley thinks so too, and although there's no time set aside to develop another song, he shows the new lyrics to Ked and Camille, gives Lexie the thumbs up and herds us all back to the studio. Fuelled by chocolate brownies and a couple of pitchers of lemonade, we play around with chords and melodies for the second new song. Camille suggests tempo changes and a different key that shifts everything and makes us all sit up and take notice. Bex begins a steady bass beat in the background while Dylan tries a couple of percussion ideas.

'I like this,' Ked says. 'Strong imagery, strong idea. And I like where you're going with the sounds too – it's different, it's good. You can go loud with this one. Layer in some subtle stuff too, but push the basic melody as hard as you can because that hook is great. I think we're on to something!'

We work on the new song all afternoon, polishing, perfecting, switching things round until we can all see the magic. There's an energy in the studio I haven't seen since we first got together, and it's infectious. It doesn't feel pressured or stressful, just exciting – a bunch of us working hard to create the best possible outcome – and I'm on a high because the song is inspired by my idea sheet from Saturday and the discussion earlier. It's something I can really relate to. For once I don't feel self-conscious or worried, I'm just part of the team, belting out the lyrics, letting Camille suggest different ways of doing it, experimenting, having fun.

Fun. That's something that's been missing from my life for a while . . . it's great to have it back again. Maybe Jake is right and this time at Fox Hollow Hall will fill us with new enthusiasm for the Lost & Found. Maybe it can repair my battered self-esteem after all?

As the rest of the band plough on with practice, Camille works with Marley, Romy, Lexie and me to develop harmonies for the two new songs. As I sing, the others weave harmonies around me. We've learned more in the last few days than we had in months working on our own.

'This is what I want from you, Sasha,' Camille tells me, grinning. 'Your voice is beautiful, but it's only now I'm hearing the passion and confidence I knew was there all along. You can't fake it. When you're singing, you need to believe the song – you need to *be* it. Keep singing like this and you'll knock the socks off Lola Rockett!'

'What did I say, Sasha?' Marley crows. 'I knew you hadn't lost your spark – I knew you could do it! I told the others it was just a blip!'

He beams at me, elated, but I can feel the smile sliding from my face. A blip? Romy and Lexie look embarrassed, awkward. They've been discussing me behind my back, discussing whether I'd lost my spark . . . Everyone but me. My skin floods with heat and shame.

Marley barges on, oblivious. 'These new songs . . . I'm telling you, they're red hot!' he declares. 'I can feel it . . . this is our breakthrough moment! We're so, so close!'

Suddenly they're all staring at me, frowning, and I know there's been another black-hole moment. I take a step backwards, confused.

'. . . hear me? Sasha?'

'Sasha? What's wrong? Are you OK?'

'This is what happened the other night, right?'

'It's happened a few times, actually. She just blanks out . . .'

Shame swamps me, snapping my new-found confidence clean in two.

I don't belong. The Lost & Found is a beautiful, crazy jigsaw of people – everybody brings their own skill and passion to the mix. Even Matt, wandering around in the background with his camera and his sarcastic smile, somehow fits in here.

I don't. No matter how hard I try, I never will.

Mask.

Make me a mask so I can be
The person that I want to be.
Make it pretty and make it bright
To keep the real me out of sight.

Make me look better than before,
Make me the same but so much more,
Make me the girl I'd like to be . . .
Make me strong and make me free.

Make me a mask so I can hide
The feelings that I keep inside.
Wipe away the guilt and shame
Give me the courage to play the game.

Make me a mask that looks like me,
To hide behind, so none can see
The broken girl behind the smile,
The girl who's been lost for quite a while.

But hide-and-seek is a lonely game
Perhaps I'll wait when you call my name
Perhaps I'll trust that this could be . . .
You don't see the mask, you just see me.

20

Watch Me Disappear

Jake takes my hand and leads me out into the dusk.

'You've all worked hard,' I can hear Ked saying inside. 'Let's call it a day for now, OK? Take a break.'

Cool air washes over me, and I can smell distant woodsmoke as I follow Jake across the grass. 'Where are we going?'

'Apple picking,' he says, as if it were obvious. 'We had a plan, right?'

'But it's almost dark!'

'Got a torch on my phone,' Jake says.

'We don't have anything to put them in!'

206

'Are you looking for trouble?' he asks. 'I have it all worked out. You'll see. Where's your sense of adventure?'

I almost laugh. 'Back in the studio, in tatters, along with my self-esteem and my short-lived career as a singer,' I say. 'You must really like apple crumble, huh?'

'I really, really like it,' he confirms. 'And I really, really like you, Sasha. So this is, like, my ideal date – not that it is a date or anything, because I probably don't have the guts to ask . . .'

'I think you just did!' I counter.

He laughs. 'Did you say yes?'

'I'm here, aren't I?' I say.

Jake halts beside a red wheelbarrow leaning against the perimeter wall. He lets go of my hand and I feel bereft suddenly, following as he steers the barrow towards the apple trees. 'Loads of fruit, see?' he says, shining his torch app into the branches.

He reaches up and starts to pick, and after a moment I join him. There is something very calming and satisfying about picking apples in the dark, the sharp smell of them, the smooth weight of them as I gently tug them loose.

'Your career isn't in tatters,' Jake says quietly. 'People are just worried about you, that's all.'

'You think Marley wants a lead singer who blanks out every few minutes?' I reply. 'I don't think so, Jake. And Marley cares way more about the band than he does about me. If I can't sing, if he can't rely on me . . . I'm out.'

Jake sighs. 'You're jumping way ahead,' he argues. 'You know what I think – you need to see a doctor, get this checked. It could be something simple, a virus or something . . .'

'I looked it up on the internet,' I say. 'Zone-out moments. It's something that can happen with stress and depression, apparently. Lucky me!'

Jake pushes the wheelbarrow along to the next tree and we start picking again. 'I don't think you're doing this to yourself,' he says. 'And I don't think you should diagnose yourself using the internet, either. That's what we've got doctors for.'

'I don't want to go to the doctor,' I say in a small voice. 'I'm scared. What if it's something bad? Something awful? What if it's not a medical thing at all?'

Jake blinks at me in the twilight. 'What else could it be?'

I try for a grin. 'I might be a time traveller, checking in from the past or the future,' I tell him. 'Or an alien from

another dimension. Maybe I'm being pulled back there by forces beyond my control . . .'

He takes a moment to suss that I'm joking, but when he does he throws his head back and laughs, raking a hand through his hair. 'What are you doing hanging out with me, then?' he asks.

'Researching human intelligence,' I say. 'You're a case study!'

'How am I doing?'

'Primitive life form,' I quip. 'Obsessed with lighting rigs and chocolate limes and after-dark apple picking. Quite kind, though. Likes to share.'

'That's a blatant hint,' he says, offering me the packet of chocolate limes. 'Who exactly is obsessed with these? I think it's you!'

I take a sweet, unwrap it and pop it into my mouth, the sharp lime flavour making my tongue curl. 'You're not taking me seriously,' I say. 'Maybe I'm some kind of girl wizard? Maybe my owl got lost on the way to deliver my invitation to Hogwarts, and I'm stuck in Muggle world trying to get by, and I don't even know I have special powers?'

Jake shakes his head, grinning, and pushes the barrow on once more. It's filling up, but we keep picking.

'What if it is something weird?' I press. 'What if I'm being possessed by some sort of evil spirit? What if I'm actually a werewolf or a vampire and don't really understand that I am? When Halloween comes, I'll reach my full power and get a whole TV series of my own . . .'

'I'll be your number-one fan,' Jake says. 'But you need to work on the facial hair and the fangs. You're not fooling anyone right now.'

I growl and claw at Jake, but he just laughs.

I sigh. 'Honestly, though. What if I'm falling into black holes and somehow crossing into a parallel universe? What if I'm travelling through time? What if there's another world somewhere and I'm a ghost, spooking people and then vanishing without trace?'

'I think you have a brilliant imagination,' he says. 'But I bet you anything there's a rational explanation for all this. Go to the doctor's when we get home . . . promise?'

A part of me acknowledges that I have to do something about the zone-out moments, that I have to keep the promise. Jake's not smiling now, and I know that

underneath all the joking around he's worried for me –
really worried.

'I'll come with you,' he says. 'Not that I don't trust you
or anything . . .'

'You can trust me,' I say, and suddenly I'm aware that we're
both standing very still, very close, alone under the apple trees
as darkness folds in around us. My heart is thumping hard
and my cheeks are warm in spite of the cold air.

'You can trust me too,' he says, and suddenly he leans
forward and kisses me, a kiss that tastes of chocolate limes
and laughter. It's not rough or pushy or damp, and there
is no hint of tuna pasta. It's shy and sweet and gentle. This
time my heart is racing for all the right reasons.

'Definitely not a werewolf,' he says softly as we break apart.
'Possibly an alien, though. That was out of this world . . .'

'Do all humans have such a cheesy sense of humour, or
just you?' I tease.

'I'm pretty unique,' he says.

He takes my hand, and it feels like a lifeline.

'That's probably enough apples,' I say, looking down at
the barrow, which is almost overflowing. 'For a lifetime or
two . . .'

'There are quite a few of us,' Jake points out. 'And you can never really have too much apple crumble.'

We kiss again, just to check that the first time wasn't a fluke. It wasn't, so we sit down on the loaded barrow and check again, just to be sure. Time slides past, and when I look up through the branches the sky is dark velvet sprinkled with stars.

'We're probably missing tea,' Jake says. 'Sheddie mentioned something about a chip shop run . . . and then we're supposed to have a progress meeting. I had some ideas. Shall we head back?'

'Race you,' I say, but we don't run. We're in no hurry. We dawdle back to the house taking turns to push and ride on the barrow. We walk so slowly that all the chips are gone by the time we reach the house. Neither of us cares, not one bit.

We walk in on a band meeting in the living room, with Ked, Camille and the Lost & Found scattered around the room discussing the new EP and the promo video. I try to pretend nothing's wrong – let's face it, I've had plenty of practice.

'Are you OK?' Lexie whispers as Jake and I sit down. 'When you blanked out earlier on – well, we were worried!'

'I'm fine!' I say brightly. 'It's just something that happens sometimes when I'm tired. It's not a problem.'

Lexie frowns, unconvinced, but she can see I don't want to talk about this and she doesn't challenge me. Nor does anyone else.

It's been decided that the two new songs will form our EP and that 'Watch Me Disappear' will be our debut single.

'All your energy has to go into this song,' Ked tells us. 'I have a good feeling about this, but it has to be perfect. Make sure you know it inside out – but we can't lose the rawness, either, the energy. Every single one of you needs to give your best!'

Marley, Dylan, Lee and Bex shoot furtive glances in my direction, and the others seem to be trying too hard not to look at me. Ked might have a good feeling, but my band mates clearly don't.

Anxiety curls in my belly. I loved singing the new songs earlier, sure, but I don't know if I can recapture that passion, not when I keep messing up, blanking out. Not when I know that the smallest imperfection matters. Not when I know I don't belong here.

My friends are trading ideas for the video Ked wants us to shoot, ideas about masks and face paint, about autumn leaves and trees and wild open landscapes, with the band wearing overcoats and scarves. The atmosphere is electric, but I feel I'm viewing it from behind glass.

The wood-burning stove is stacked with logs and belting out a lot of heat. The room feels stifling suddenly, and I lean back against Jake, feeling hot and bothered and disconnected.

I've tried so hard for so long to be what the Lost & Found want me to be, need me to be, but tonight I somehow can't do it any more. It's like someone has pulled the plug and cut off the power supply.

I'm flatlining, failing.

'You OK, Sash?' Jake whispers, frowning. He moves a little nearer, slides an arm round my waist. If anyone thinks it strange that we're sitting so close, they don't say so, and I'm grateful for that. It should feel safe, it should feel cool – but I'm drifting now, lost.

'What d'you think, Sasha?' Romy asks at one point, and I realize someone's asked me a question and I've missed it completely.

'Sorry . . . think I'm too tired to be any use here,' I say. 'It's been a long day . . . a cool day . . . but I've got a headache and I think I'll have an early night. I want to be OK for tomorrow!'

'Want a paracetamol?' Camille asks. 'Take the edge off the pain?'

'It always helps my migraines,' Mandy chips in, concerned. 'A dab of lavender on your pillow can help too. I might have some in my bag, if you think . . .'

'No, no, I just need to sleep,' I promise. 'I'll be fine, honest!'

I get up to leave, Jake following, and I see Romy's eyebrows shoot up, notice Lexie whispering something to Sami and Happi. They seem to have sussed me and Jake, but it's no big deal – the chat starts up again as we go into the kitchen, because everyone is wired and fizzing with ideas, everyone except me.

I try not to care too much.

'Hot chocolate is the best cure,' Jake says, rummaging in the cupboard above the kettle and extracting a couple of mugs.

'For what?'

'For tired girls who like to time travel, howl at the moon and drift through other solar systems as a hobby,' he says. 'I think I saw some squirty cream in the fridge . . .'

'How about girls who just feel out of their depth and a little bit scared?' I ask.

'Them too,' Jake says. 'And also boys who have a crush on a girl who thinks she's a time-travelling, ghostly werewolf. It's good for them too.'

'Who is this boy?' I tease. 'Do I know him?'

'Might do . . .'

'And hot chocolate is really the only cure?'

Jake grins. 'There is one other thing . . .'

He leans close and kisses the end of my nose, and suddenly I'm filled with such a tangle of happiness and sadness that my eyes brim with tears.

'Let's just stick with the hot chocolate for now,' he says. 'You need to sleep. I'm going to go back to the others. I have an idea to suggest to those stylist people. Tomorrow's going to be awesome . . . see you at eight for yoga?'

'You bet!'

'I'll go, then,' Jake says. 'We don't want to start a rumour . . .'

'Might be too late for that!' I grin, and I cradle my hot chocolate and head into the darkened hall.

A couple of lamps at the foot of the sweeping staircase throw out gentle pools of light, so I don't bother to put the main light on, just tread softly up the stairs, trying not to spill my drink. On the landing it's darker, and I'm startled to see a shadow coming towards me from the left, a tall figure that halts abruptly. My heart races in alarm until I realize the shadowy figure is Matt.

'Hello?' I say warily. 'Matt? What are you doing, creeping about in the dark? You just about made me jump out of my skin!'

'Could ask you the exact same question,' he says. 'And if you don't put the light on, you can't complain about the dark, can you?'

I frown. 'Look, I'm tired . . . it's been a long day and I need an early night. You scared me for a minute, that's all. What were you doing, anyway? We're supposed to stay away from Ked's private rooms, aren't we?'

'I took a wrong turning,' Matt says. 'Easily done in a house this big.'

'I suppose . . .'

217

It's not a mistake anyone else has made, though. I can't help noticing the camera hanging round his neck and wonder if Matt's telling the truth or if he's been sneaking around Ked's rooms in search of something that could win him his big break as a journalist.

I shake my head to push away the thought. Matt is ambitious and determined, sure, but he wouldn't do that – would he?

Watch Me Disappear

Paint me indigo, paint me red,
Every colour in my head.
Stark, dramatic, angry, bright . . .
Every colour of the night.

Paint a face the world can see,
Paint a face that could be me,
But I was never here . . .
Watch me disappear.

Paint me yellow, paint me white,
Colours of the morning light.
Sharp, unflinching, crystal clear,
Colours that might hide my fear.

Paint a face the world can see,
Paint a face that could be me.
I was never here,
Watch me disappear.

Paint me green and paint me blue,
Every single daylight hue.
Fresh and natural, bright and clean,
Colours that make sure I'm seen.

Paint a face the world can see,
Paint a face that could be me.
I'm not really here,
Watch me disappear.

Paint me every rainbow shade,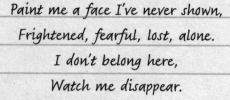
Colours that will never fade.
Every colour, every hue,
Bright and dark and soft and true.

Paint me a face I've never shown,
Frightened, fearful, lost, alone.
I don't belong here,
Watch me disappear.

21

Magic

I fall asleep at dawn and dream that I'm a space traveller, a time traveller, a ghost, a lone wolf howling at the moon. I've missed yoga, and Romy and the others are nowhere to be seen, but thankfully no wolfish fur or pointed teeth are visible as I do my make-up in the bathroom mirror.

I grab a cereal bar for breakfast – Mrs B is still missing – and head for my vocal coaching session with Camille, but although I try my hardest I can tell she's looking for something more.

'Let go, Sasha,' she tells me. 'Give it everything you've got!'

I'm giving everything I have and then some, but even I know something is missing. Camille is looking for a repeat

of yesterday's moment of magic; she's looking for miracles and I'm fresh out of those.

Outside the window I see a little white van draw up on the gravel. Ria and Fitz jump out, unloading crates and boxes and cases to carry into the house, ready to help create our new look. I can't help wishing I was with them, lugging boxes and wielding a make-up palette, instead of in here singing scales and voice exercises and making Camille sigh.

'Focus, Sasha,' she says. 'Concentrate!'

And then I vanish again.

I know because the backing track has somehow jumped forward, and my mind is struggling to remember what I'm supposed to be singing, and I'm staring out of the window at the place where the van was parked a few moments ago, but isn't any longer.

Camille is looking at me sadly.

'OK, OK,' she says. 'We'll stop there for today. I won't lie to you, sweetheart, I'm worried. Something's going on here, and it's not just daydreaming. Want to tell me about it?'

I can't meet her eyes. 'It just happens,' I say. 'I can't control it. It's why I'm so scared about being on stage. I'm

the lead singer – everyone's focused on me, and if it happens at a concert . . . well, that doesn't bear thinking about.'

'You're saying this is something you can't control?' she checks. 'That you just – well, freeze – at any time?'

I nod and the tears I've been pushing away blur my vision and roll slowly down my cheeks. 'I don't even know it's happened until afterwards . . . and everyone just assumes I'm being dozy or awkward or downright rude. It's horrible!'

'Oh, sweetheart,' Camille says, handing me a tissue. 'I'm not sure what's going on, but I guarantee there'll be a logical explanation for it. I'll have a word with Ked, see what he thinks. Whatever happens, you mustn't let this get to you!'

'Don't tell him,' I plead. 'He'll be so angry . . . Marley too!'

'Of course they won't,' she says. 'Look, I'd like to get you checked by a doctor, make sure there's nothing going on we should be worried about. This has to be sorted, Sasha. I can't imagine the worry you're carrying, trying to keep this secret and pretend you're OK, but it's time to be brave now, find out what's wrong and get it treated. You're an

amazing girl, but you can't front a rising indie pop band with something like this going on. I think you know that.'

I nod, silent, choked.

'Ked needs to know. Perhaps his doctor can check you out and get this sorted. Let's hope so!'

'Please don't,' I whisper, but Camille just shakes her head, and I know that the time for hiding is past.

I've done such a good job of ignoring my black-hole episodes, but no matter what I do they won't go away. They just keep happening over and over. Everyone will notice in the end – this thing will unravel my school life, my friendships. It will unravel everything.

I tilt my chin up, the way I always do, and try to ignore the prickle of tears in my eyes.

Fitz and Ria are like creatures from another planet – a cooler, weirder, more colourful planet – and they have transformed the music room into an Aladdin's cave of possibility. Peeping round the door, I see rails of clothes in bright colours and rich fabrics, tall mirrors propped against the walls, trestle tables laden with more make-up than I've ever seen. And, trust me, I have seen a lot.

Jake grins and waves as he helps to set up the projector, and I can't help smiling as I watch him check the sound, making sure Fitz and Ria are happy. This is one bit of the schedule I've been looking forward to – it's about helping us find a look for the band, and after meeting Fitz and Ria at Starshine, I can't wait to see what they've come up with.

'You're amazing,' Ria tells us, once we're all inside and sprawled across the squashy sofas that face the stage. 'You're young, you look great, you have personality and individuality. What you need now is something to pull you together. Think of the iconic bands and solo artists of the past. They all had a strong look, an image, that helped them stand out from the crowd. Since meeting the band at Starshine we've been in constant touch with some of you, exchanging ideas and concepts. We're really excited about the new image and the promo video – let's show you what we have in mind!'

Jake flicks a switch and images appear on the white wall behind the stage while a rough cut of our new song, 'Watch Me Disappear', plays softly in the background. It's mesmerizing. A carousel of perfectly made-up faces plays before us, dramatic eyes lined in black, false lashes like spiders, dark lips, hair gelled and backcombed like something from a horror film. The clothes are raggedy layers of different fabrics and textures, all in black. The images morph gradually into vintage shots of sixties models, wide-eyed and innocent with pixie crops or long tumbling hair, in short dresses and skinny jeans, baggy shirts and waistcoats.

'That's Louisa Winter!' Lexie says, as a couple of images of the artist flash up on screen – photos from her modelling days long ago.

She looks beautiful, luminous, full of life.

'We looked for inspiration from eighties and nineties emo-goth style, because your songs are very emotional and intense,' Fitz says, as the series of slides ends and then begins again. 'Then we added in some sixties youth and simplicity – that's also a strong theme in your music. We want to mix the two – big eyes, wild hair, dark clothes, with a sixties vibe of wide-eyed innocence.'

'Have you met Marley Hayes?' Bex quips, and everyone laughs. '"Innocent" is not the word that springs to mind!'

'Looks can be deceptive,' Marley argues.

226

Dylan chucks a cushion at him, and our focus turns back to the screen.

'Last night, Ked emailed a SoundCloud link for your new songs,' Fitz goes on. 'We *loved* them – the imagery, the message, it's all so brilliantly *you*. We've chatted to the film crew about their video, and we had the idea of showing you all in monochrome for the live performance, then introducing colour for the outside shots. Jake has put together a slide show of your ideas too, and, as you'll see, they fit beautifully with what we had in mind. I'd like to invite Bex and Lexie up to explain.'

Bex and Lexie come forward, but Jake stays safely behind the projector as the new slides begin to play. We're looking at a chaos of images that could have been taken at the Hindu festival of Holi, the one where everyone throws coloured powder at each other. The images are joyful, powerful, moving – I can see just how well this idea could work with our new songs.

Bex glances up at the slide show. 'We had a lot of ideas,' she says. 'From painting each other with brushes and poster paint to hiding our faces – our new songs are very visual, and it makes sense to use their imagery in the video. We loved the idea of the film cutting between shots of us performing to scenes of us in the woods at Fox Hollow Hall with paint and brushes, messing around. The contrast of monochrome and colour would be awesome!'

'We're putting together a sort of script – a film sequence, I suppose,' Lexie says. 'The face-paint idea would start off gently, then get wilder – eventually we'd be throwing around coloured powder, getting it in our hair and all over our clothes . . .'

'Which would work really well with our plan for neutral-coloured clothes,' Fitz says, grinning.

'Exactly,' Bex agrees. 'Jake had the idea of projecting coloured lights on to the band as they play too, starting in monochrome and working up to a kaleidoscope of colour as the song builds. We'll add the colour gradually, cutting between shots of us performing and shots playing with paint, and we want to use Sasha as the focus of all this.'

She looks at me for approval, and I wish I'd listened more last night and hadn't gone to bed early, because I don't like where this is going, not at all.

'You're the lead singer, obviously,' she says to me. 'The face of the band . . .'

228

Panic flutters inside my chest. I don't want to be the face of the band. I don't even want to be the lead singer, not if I'm honest with myself – and admitting that, even to myself, is terrifying.

Lexie takes over again. 'We thought one of the first cutaway shots could show Sasha having her make-up done . . . a perfectly made-up face,' she explains. 'Later, she'll have handprints and brushmarks of bright colours covering that up, then showers of coloured powder to camouflage it all – lots of close-ups. And the end shot will be Sasha wiping away all the make-up and paint to reveal her true face – but when she looks at the camera for her final close-up, we'll see a face with eyes rimmed with black, like a ghost, her face icy-pale, her lips white – maybe twigs and spiders and remnants of the coloured powder in her tangled hair . . .'

A twist of nausea rises inside me, and I wish I could fall into a black hole right now.

'Wow,' Ria is saying. 'Powerful – I can totally imagine!'

'It's like she's revealing the fear and the darkness inside,' Bex concludes. 'Which is sort of what the song is about. Well, those were our ideas, anyway!'

229

I wrap my arms round myself to try to hold myself together, but I can feel I'm coming apart even so. I can feel myself melting, crumbling, breaking up.

Ked is talking now, telling us he knew we had potential but he didn't know just how much talent and creativity we had. 'OK Film are coming over tonight to finalize ideas – they'll love this, I know. We've got this afternoon and all day tomorrow to get the songs recorded, leaving Thursday for styling and filming. With any luck, we can get the single released mid-November, with a big splash in the media to support it. If we're lucky, Lola Rockett will get behind it too, and I don't have to tell you what that could mean. Good work, everyone! I'll leave you with Ria and Fitz for a make-up and styling dress rehearsal.'

Jake shuts down the slide show and the lights come up. I push my fears away, fix on the brightest smile I can muster, stand up and walk towards the make-up table.

'Wow,' I breathe. 'All these bottles and jars and paints and potions . . . I feel like the sorcerer's apprentice!'

'You're right,' Ria says with a smile. 'There's magic in these bottles and jars! Shall we do you first? I never did get round to that makeover at Starshine, did I?'

I'm sitting in the fancy swivel chair, while Ria chats easily as she swipes primer, foundation and shader on to my face. She outlines my eyes with smudgy kohl and snips an extravagant false eyelash into halves to attach to the outer edges of my eyes. Cobalt blue and turquoise and jade, glittery white . . . Ria picks colours I'd never dare try in real life. She paints my lips the palest pink, dusts sparkles along my cheekbones and twirls the chair round to face the mirror.

I don't recognize the girl looking back at me. Her long blonde hair has been brushed into long curtains, her eyes are huge and her skin is pale and flawless. She looks young and innocent yet somehow fierce and proud and strong. She's like some kind of alien princess . . . but she's me.

'See? Magic!' Ria says.

'I love it!' I whisper. 'I mean, I really, really love it. Thank you! How did you get into this career? Did you have to go to college?'

Ria grins. 'There are plenty of courses,' she tells me. 'Beauty therapy, make-up, special effects . . . but, actually, I did a fashion degree – it's where I met Fitz. I found I was more interested in styling and doing the make-up for shoots and shows – I like designing faces more than I like designing clothes! No formal training as such, just a real passion for what I do.'

A barrage of flashes go off in my face. 'Look at the camera,' Matt is saying. 'Tilt your head back . . . now to one side . . . try to look happy . . .'

More flashes. Matt barks out his demands and I play along, pretending it's somehow fun. I can't help wondering why I ever thought Matt was cute. He's bossy and sarcastic, his eyes cold, lips scornful. I must have been mad to think I was falling for him.

I sneak a glance at Jake, at the back of the room playing with the light filters, projecting colours above our heads on to the screen behind the stage. I like the way he chews his lip when he's concentrating, the way his hair sticks up in several directions like it hasn't seen a comb in days, even though I'm pretty sure he gels it carefully every morning. I like the way his blue eyes scan the room for me every few minutes, the way he grins at me when he thinks nobody's watching.

I like Jake.

'Ready to pick some clothes?' Fitz asks, steering me towards the rails of black and grey garments. 'Choose some opaque tights and boots, a scarf for your hair – and try on these dresses so we can see which looks best.'

I scoop up a selection of clothes and take them to the nearest loo to change, shimmying into dove-grey tights, flat black op-art boots and a black minidress with strange bell-like sleeves. I put the scarf in my hair and laugh because I look so ridiculous.

'Too heavy, too blocky,' Fitz decides, as I step out to show him. 'And the scarf isn't working, is it?'

The second dress is a sleeveless grey shift with a faint paisley print. It looks much better, but Fitz still isn't sure. Try the last one,' he tells me. 'We have to get this right!'

The last outfit is a loose grey slash-neck jumper worn with a tiny black suedette skirt, accessorized with a hoop-link belt and a floppy hat.

'That is the one,' Fitz announces. 'I knew it!'

And when I go back into the music room, people turn their heads to look. The girls tell me I look amazing and even Marley seems pleased. I begin to wonder if I can do this, if fronting a band is just a matter of finding a good enough disguise and being brave?

Then I remember my blackout moments, and I know I'm kidding myself. I'm wasting everybody's time.

I take a deep breath in and act my part a little bit harder, even so.

My friends are getting ready. Lexie and Romy have reprised their glittery look from Sunday, and Marley is stalking around with kohl-rimmed eyes, Chelsea boots, skinny jeans and a black-and-grey tie-dye T-shirt. Ria is transforming Bex, who can't quite decide whether to be against all make-up on feminist grounds, or to cut loose and get Ria to use every colour on offer. 'Make me look fierce,' she decides at last. 'That'd be pretty empowering, right?'

'Can you help us for a bit, Sasha?' Ria asks, flustered. 'Before we run out of time?'

I don't have to be asked twice. I take a moment to mix and match a base colour for Happi, then highlight with glitter and shade her eyes with gold and green. With her hair twisted up into two tiny buns sprinkled with stars, Happi looks amazing.

'Stunning, Sasha,' Ria says. 'Remember, if things don't work out with the Lost & Found, just give me a call – you can intern for me and Fitz any time!'

'I will,' I say, beaming with pride as Fitz whisks Happi away to be dressed and Dylan flops down in the chair for his turn. 'I'd love that!'

I sponge on some base to hide Dylan's spots and some colour to highlight his cheekbones, and find myself wishing I really could do this for a living. It'd be so cool – getting a bride ready for her big day, or an actor ready to be filmed, or a model ready for her photo shoot. Maybe I do have a talent?

I see Jake in the background, carrying boxes, setting up the ironing board, helping to iron a pile of sixties shirts and T-shirts to hang on one of the rails.

'Poor Jake, stuck with the ironing,' Dylan says, grabbing a trilby hat and a feather boa as Fitz marches past with an armful of accessories. 'He misses out on all the fun stuff!'

But I don't think Jake is missing out. He has the buzz of being part of the Lost & Found without the stress, and that's what I'd like too. 'Stop wriggling,' I tell Dylan, then I dust him with powder and set him loose for Fitz to adorn.

What Ria and Fitz do is a kind of alchemy – with a few paints, powders and vintage finds they have transformed us all, given us an identity we didn't have before. We look amazing – we look like a band, and I can visualize how much more amazing we'll be when we're let loose with the paints and coloured powder for the video.

And now Ria and Fitz are packing up to leave, instructing us to hang up our costumes ready for Thursday once Matt's through with us. It's photo-shoot time.

Instead of a formal photocall, Matt wants us to clown around beside the clothes rails with guitars and hats and shawls. He fires off a few shots, the flash on repeat, then ushers us through to the kitchen where Mandy and Jon are setting out a lunch of pizza slices and chunky chips.

Matt snaps us sitting on, at and in front of the table, eating pizza, and then messing about with ladles, oven gloves and a fish slice beside the scarlet Aga. Finally, he clumps us together against the blue and yellow Moroccan-tiled wall, eating chips and laughing as he fires the flash over and over again.

It's exciting and fun and I'm laughing along with the others . . . and then I'm not.

Black hole, a blur of faces, black hole again.

'. . . are you even listening, Sasha?' Matt's angry voice cuts through the confusion in my head. 'Is it too much to

236

ask you to smile? Look at the camera? Or are you really as bored as you look?'

'I . . . what?' I say.

Matt lowers the camera, clearly annoyed.

'It's like photographing a plank of wood!' he grumbles. 'What is it with you? D'you think you're too good for the rest of the band? You're not a superstar yet, you know!'

I frown, trying to untangle the accusations. 'I don't . . . That's not what I think!'

'Leave it,' Romy says, stepping up beside me. 'Seriously, Matt. Shouting isn't going to help!'

'Matt, mate, back off,' Marley adds. 'You're out of order!'

Jake steps up to my other side. 'Ignore him,' he says to me quietly. 'He's a loser . . . a jerk!'

'Can't any of you see?' Matt growls. 'She's the weak link here . . . she doesn't care about the band. Don't any of you get it?'

'Don't *you* get it, Matt?' Marley repeats coldly. 'Don't you see? Sasha's one of us.'

SashaSometimes

189 likes

SashaSometimes Want to see my new look?
#1960sVibe #MakeoverMadness #BandLife #Lost&Found

Lara_M Yes!

ZeeC YES!!!

Kezsez07 Please!

JBSings Don't keep us guessing!

PetraB Yes

Yorkie_Joe Sure do!

littlejen Is there a release date for the EP yet?

Lil_Chels You're my hero, Sasha!

22

Try Again

My friends rally round, telling me to ignore Matt, that he's jealous because I've dropped him for Jake. There may be a grain of truth in this, but deep down I know that Matt has seen what the others haven't yet – that I don't belong in the band.

The knowledge sticks in my throat, sharp and dangerous like a shard of glass.

'Marley's having a word,' Jake says, and, sure enough, I can hear the raised voices from where we're sitting, sprawled across the squashy sofas in the living room. We're all still in full costume and make-up, which is surreal. Jake's the only one who looks normal, and I'm holding his hand tightly.

'I should have thumped him,' Bex tells me. 'Who does he think he is, anyway?'

'A jumped-up posh boy with a ruthless streak a mile wide?' Jake suggests.

'Maybe he just gets really easily stressed?' Lexie is saying. 'Still, he had no right to have a go at you like that, Sash. Don't let it get to you!'

'You try to see the best in everyone, Lexie,' Happi comments. 'But maybe it's like Jake says, and Matt's just not very nice? And he is totally jealous because Sash turned him down!'

'I don't think I like him much,' Sami agrees.

'Don't think any of us do,' Lee chips in.

I bite my lip. 'I honestly don't think I'm better than anyone else.'

'We know that,' Bex says. 'Obviously!'

'I know I haven't been at my best this week. I haven't been sleeping, and sometimes when I'm tired I just blank out a bit . . .'

Jake raises an eyebrow, but I can't meet his eye. He doesn't get it. How do you tell your friends you're blanking out half a dozen times a day, and that it's not just a quiet, daydreamy moment but a total black-hole experience, when you lose yourself and everything else as well? How do you tell your friends you can't be what they need you to be, that you're going to let them down big style, sooner rather than later?

I can't. The Lost & Found means a lot to me, but it means even more to the kids sitting around me. It's their hopes, their dreams, their future. I have to keep trying, pretending things are OK, because the alternative just doesn't bear thinking about.

'I love my makeover,' Happi tells me, determined to get me smiling. 'I couldn't believe it when I looked in the mirror. You even made Dylan look half human!'

'Oi!' Dylan objects. 'I'm naturally good-looking, I'll have you know! Although . . . it's Halloween at the weekend, isn't it? Sasha could give us all scary makeovers.'

'I like the idea of that,' Lexie says. 'We could have a Halloween band practice or go trick or treating!'

'Or a Halloween party at the old railway carriage?' Bex suggests. 'Reckon we'll have earned some chill time!'

'Yeah, Sasha can make us look super scary,' Jake adds. 'Face paint and fake blood . . . and this time I get to be transformed too!'

I grin. My friends have found a way to pull me back into the group, put me at the centre of things, and I am grateful.

There are no raised voices in the kitchen now. Marley bounds into the room, grinning, to tell us that he's sorted Matt out, that there won't be any more trouble. He must have done a quick change too, because he's back in his jeans and jumper, although the eyeliner and glitter remains.

'Matt's OK, really,' he insists. 'He's just a perfectionist. It's probably hard for him as an outsider – he doesn't understand how close we all are.'

I don't think I understood, either, but I do now. I also know that Matt has done a job on Marley, spun a line and grabbed himself a second chance. I guess the promise of publicity is hard for Marley to resist.

'Anyway, Sash, he won't give you any more trouble – I guarantee it,' Marley says. 'I've told him to back off, do something else for the afternoon. He's going for a walk to

sort his head out. And he's going to apologize. I told him that was non-negotiable.'

I smile weakly. I can imagine how thrilled Matt must be about that.

'So,' Marley continues. 'We're recording in the studio this afternoon, and it needs to be perfect, so let's put this out of our heads and focus on the music. That's what we're here for, yeah?'

'Definitely,' we all chorus.

'Thanks, Marley,' I tack on to the end of this. 'For sticking up for me.'

He grins. 'No worries. And if we work hard this afternoon, we deserve a break. How about we go swimming straight after recording? Relax a bit? And then we'll be all set to meet the film crew dudes at dinner.'

'Now you're talking,' Lee says. 'We can get the Jacuzzi working . . .'

'And try out the sauna and the steam room!' Dylan adds.

'And actually have some fun,' Lexie agrees. 'We've earned it!'

Marley grins. 'Cool. Now, remember we need these clothes for the video shoot, and Fitz wanted everything hung up again. Push off and get changed, and grab your swimming stuff for later, so we can head over straight from the studio. Quick! I don't care if you leave the make-up on, but the costumes have to be on that rail, pristine. See you in the studio in ten, ready to knock the socks off Ked and Camille! Scram!'

We work all afternoon on the first of the two new songs, 'Mask', but when it comes to knocking the socks off Ked and Camille, I'm not quite managing it. Our mentors seem happy with the trumpet solo, the violin melodies, the drum and bass. They love Sami's haunting flute and George's cello melody, even the harmonies that Lexie and Happi have created. They just don't like my vocals.

I'm in a glass-walled sound booth with a huge, flat mic in front of my face and headphones on my ears so I can hear the basic soundtrack as I sing. It feels weird and awkward and unnatural.

'We can make as many recordings as it takes,' Camille says. 'The vocals need to be strong, pure, spot on. They'll carry the track.'

No pressure then.

'Try again,' Ked tells me. 'From the top!'

I focus. I think of all the vocal coaching I've had from Camille, her breathing techniques, her tips on projection and pacing and power. I give it everything I've got.

'Again,' Ked says.

I try again and again and again, and in the end Ked wanders off to talk to Marley, a frown creasing his face.

'Let loose,' Camille tells me. 'I want to see the energy, the passion you gave us yesterday. Get into the song, into the heart of it. Don't worry about being perfect – just give me the passion!'

But today I can't get past the twist of failure in my gut, the panic that builds with every breath. I can't find the magic no matter how hard I try.

'OK,' Camille declares at last. 'Enough. Have an early night, Sasha, and we'll try again in the morning.'

I try not to let my shame show.

'Good work, people,' Ked says. 'We have some brilliant stuff, and we have all day tomorrow to add the final touches and get "Watch Me Disappear" down. You've all worked really hard!'

His eyes slide over me, as if he can't quite include me in this praise, and my heart aches.

'Swimming pool, everyone!' Marley reminds us. 'Got your costumes? Let's go!'

I trail after the others, Jake falling into step beside me.

'OK?' he checks, and I tell him I'm struggling, that Ked and Camille weren't happy with my vocals today.

'How come?' he asks. 'It sounded good to me.'

'Good isn't enough,' I explain. 'Whatever it is they're looking for, I don't think I can deliver it.'

'You're too hard on yourself,' Jake says. 'C'mon, let's have some downtime. Got your swim stuff?'

'I left it on my bed,' I realize. 'I'm not sure, though – what if it's not a good idea? What if I zone out in the water? That could be dangerous . . .'

'You'll be with me,' Jake says, taking my hand. 'And afterwards we're making apple crumble for the gang, right? It'll be fun!'

He fixes me with his lopsided grin, and just for a moment it feels like this is all that matters . . . holding hands with a cute boy, having a laugh with friends, living in the moment. But it's hard to live in the moment when you keep losing

chunks of it. My life is like one of those thousand-piece jigsaw puzzles you find at the back of a cupboard, one with so many pieces missing there's no way of making sense of it. The kind of jigsaw puzzle that's good only for the bin.

I push the thought away.

'I'll fetch my stuff,' I promise Jake. 'You go on . . . I'll be five minutes.'

I run into the house through the side door and across the kitchen, head upstairs. In the bedroom, I pause to brush my hair, grab shampoo and conditioner, check my eyeliner hasn't smudged. I take a look at Mary Shelley the tortoise, basking under her heat lamp, and give her a sliver of red pepper and a dandelion leaf from the resealable box on the windowsill, then I gather up my swimming things and head downstairs.

SashaSometimes

292 likes

SashaSometimes New look!
#Lost&Found #TeenBand #SixtiesStyle #GlitterGirl

Brownie Wow, looks cool!

Kezsez07 Luv this!

OllieK Gorgeous!

SaraLou Amazing!

littlejen Too cute!

MillfordGirl1 Where's the hat from? I want one!

PetraB Adorable!

MattBFotos #SorryNotSorry

23

Something Missing

I don't mean to eavesdrop . . . that's the last thing on my mind. It's just that I hear voices in the kitchen as I start to push the door open and cut through, and the voices belong to Ked and Camille. They're talking about me.

I stop short, my heart racing. I want to step away, block my ears, rewind, but I'm rooted to the spot. I can't help myself. I hear it all.

'. . . definitely an issue,' Camille says. 'Now that I've noticed it, I can see her blanking out four or five times a day. More, maybe. She's in denial, of course. She really didn't want me to tell you, but I'm worried about her, Ked. I don't think she's well.'

'We should have got her to the doctor's the other evening,' Ked says. 'What d'you think it is? Stress? Panic attacks? Some kind of seizure?'

'She says it's exhaustion,' Camille answers. 'She's not sleeping, she's anxious, she's driving herself really hard . . . she's a great kid, I like her a lot, but the fact is she can't front a band if she's ill. It's a worry.'

'Agreed,' he says. 'But I think we both know that the blanking out is only part of the problem. She has a great voice, she works hard, she's a really pretty girl . . . but the truth is, there's something missing.'

I put a hand against the door, try to steady my breathing. The world blurs and falls away, comes back, vanishes again.

'. . . the timing couldn't be worse, but I suppose it's better to know now rather than later . . .'

'Looks like we might have some tough decisions to make.'

I stumble away from the door and retrace my steps to the bedroom. Tears snake down my cheeks as I pull my little wheelie case from the bottom of the wardrobe and stuff in my things. My tread is soft and silent as I creep back down the stairs and along the hallway. I pass the kitchen where Ked and Camille are still discussing my uselessness and head to the front door, closing it softly behind me.

The light is starting to fade as I look out across the grounds of Fox Hollow Hall, scanning the woodland, the lawn, the distant studio. My friends are at the far end of the house, splashing around in Ked's pool, having fun. They don't know yet that I won't be joining them, or that I've smashed their dreams of stardom to pieces.

I wonder if any of them will still be speaking to me come Monday, or if they'll be angry that I kept my failings secret. Jake told me to be honest, to come clean about the zone-out moments and my doubts about the band, but I was too scared – now it's all caught up with me in the worst possible way.

Tonight OK Film are coming to discuss a video that will never be made, and tomorrow the studio is booked to record a single that will never be released. Lola Rockett will be coming to dinner tomorrow night to discuss a promising teen band that is about to go down in history as the best new band that never was . . . and it's all my fault.

As I walk down the steps and stride across the grass away from the house, raindrops begin to fall – fat, heavy raindrops that build to a downpour. Great. I drag my suitcase behind me, leaving a dark trail across the damp lawn.

'The gate's the other way,' a cynical voice calls. 'You make a habit of getting things wrong, don't you? Or maybe you're trying to sneak off without being seen. Don't tell me – running away again?'

Matt is sheltering under a tree watching me. One eyebrow quirks upward as he notices my tear-stained face, and his lip curls, caught between amusement and disdain.

'What's up?' he asks. 'Have they finally noticed that you're no good and chucked you out?'

'Something like that,' I say. 'Happy now, Matt? Is this a good enough scoop for you?'

'You're way too sensitive for a life in showbiz,' he tells me. 'And by the way, your mascara's all over your face. Not so perfect now, huh? Still, nice shot for my portfolio. Never know when it might come in handy!'

He takes the zoom lens from his pocket and attaches it smoothly, raising the camera before I have time to turn away. He fires off a volley of shots that feel as humiliating as a slap.

'I could have helped you,' he calls after me. 'I still could – give your side of the story. We could expose the pressure

252

Ked has put on the band to perform, how he's bullied and pushed you to the brink, how he treats those who don't make the grade – the ruthless side of Britain's best-loved pop legend . . .'

Matt's twisting things, inventing his own storyline. I'm upset with Ked and Camille right now, but no way would I lie about them to fit Matt's version of events. Ked's a tough taskmaster, but he has only ever been good to us, tried to help us. I've let Ked and Camille down every bit as much as I've let down the Lost & Found.

I can hear Matt's laugh and the click of the camera behind me as I drag my wheelie suitcase into the trees.

It's clear straight away that this is not a good idea. The wheels clog with fallen leaves, splatter me with mud and catch on tree roots, and the woods are dark and dank.

At last I reach the perimeter wall and throw the battered suitcase over into the lane. I scramble over the wall in its wake, ripping my scarf on a thorn bush and grazing my hand as I tear it free. I take a deep breath and gather my thoughts. Which way is the village? I can't remember, but I know it's quite a walk. I turn left and hope for the best, dragging the suitcase behind me.

Why are there no street lights in the countryside? The lane has no pavement; a couple of times I stumble into a ditch that runs along the grass verge. The adrenaline rush of escape has dulled, and feelings of anxiety and hopelessness seep in. I should have planned this better. I should have waited till morning, worked out a plan, called home. I should have thought first and then acted, but it's too late now. I can't go back.

And then I hear it, the muffled sound of someone walking in the lane behind me. I move faster, fear burning my throat like acid, but the footsteps keep coming. It's almost dark now, but not so dark I can't see the figure looming towards me.

I swipe the torch app on my phone and aim it into the darkness, heart racing. The beam lights up a familiar face.

'Jake!' I squeak, all the tension leaking out of me. 'What are you *doing*? I thought you were an axe murderer or something!'

Jake puts his hands in the air, as if to demonstrate that he has no axe concealed about his person. 'I was waiting for you and you didn't come, so I went to see what was up,' he explains. 'I bumped into Matt, who made some barbed comment about you running away again. You weren't in the grounds, so I thought I'd just take a walk down to the village in case that loser really did say something stupid to make you bolt . . .'

'It wasn't Matt,' I say. 'I mean, he is a loser, and he was shooting his mouth off, but that's not why —'

'What then?' Jake demands. 'What happened? You seemed fine, then . . . gone! And this time you mean it, by the look of you.'

He nods towards the muddy suitcase, still trailing a length of bramble.

'I do mean it,' I say, tears sliding down my cheeks. 'This whole week has been one big mistake from start to finish — I should never have come. I've messed things up for everybody and I feel awful. I'm going home. I don't belong here.'

Jake shakes his head sadly. 'Look, Sasha,' he says. 'Are you totally sure you want to leave? Whatever's upset you, there'll be a solution.'

'Trust me,' I tell him. 'There isn't!'

'We could speak to Ked . . .'

'No, Jake. I just want to go home,' I say in a small voice.

'Sure?'

'Sure.'

Fifteen minutes later we're huddled inside a ramshackle bus shelter, soaked and shivering and holding hands. 'You don't have to come with me,' I say. 'I don't want to get you into trouble. You were enjoying all the tech stuff, and you won't get to do all those cool lighting effects for the video if you do a disappearing act . . .'

'There'll be other chances,' he says. 'I can't let you go on your own.'

'You can. I'll get the next bus to . . . wherever the nearest town is, and find the railway station, and get a train home. Honestly, Jake, I can do it!'

'I know you can,' he says. 'But I'm coming anyway. Fox Hollow Hall won't be as much fun without you, and I'm not sure there'll even be a video if you've gone missing. They'll go nuts once they realize!'

A tidal wave of guilt hits me. There will be no video, no recording, no slot on primetime TV on Lola Rockett's music show for the Lost & Found now . . . not without a lead singer. I have brought disaster on my friends.

'I'm not going back,' I say. 'Don't try and guilt-trip me. I feel bad enough already!'

'No worries,' Jake says with a shrug. 'I'd quite like to hang around and watch the storm break, but on balance we're probably best out of it. They'll get over it. Things will get patched up somehow. And this'll be an adventure!'

We peer into the darkness, ever hopeful. Maybe the next bus isn't for hours? Maybe buses don't even run this late in the back of beyond? If something doesn't turn up soon, people will notice we've gone and send out a search party, and that's the very last thing I want.

'I've never run away from anything before,' I say sadly.

Jake laughs. 'Don't worry, I'm pretty much an expert, remember? I took off for a week last year . . . caused a whole lot of trouble for my mum and Sheddie, though I didn't think of that at the time. Looking back, I can see it was a mistake, but at the time I was determined. Nobody in the world could have talked me out of it, which is why I'm not trying to talk you out of it either.'

'Good!'

'But I have to tell you, some things you can't outrun no matter how hard you try . . . you know that, right? You have to face stuff sometime . . .'

'I know,' I say.

Two bright headlights sweep round the corner, and a wheezing coach rattles towards us, slows and stops.

Jake bounds up the steps and grins at the driver. 'Two tickets to Barnstaple, please,' he says confidently.

And then we're off.

You OK, Sash? You didn't come swimming, and Matt made some snarky comment about you running off, but Lexie reckons you've just gone for a moonlit walk with Jake and got stranded in the rain! Do we send out a search party? Don't forget the film crew people are coming after tea! Romy x

24

Runaways

The bus to Barnstaple bumps and rumbles its way through the dark, and while Jake gazes out of the window into the gloom, I switch my phone to selfie mode and check my make-up. My eyes are red and gritty with crying, and mascara has run in rivulets down my cheeks. I dab at the damage with a tissue, but there's not much I can do.

Abruptly, a text message from Romy pops up.

'Message?' Jake asks. 'What's it say?'

'Romy wanting to know where we are. I'm not going to answer.'

He sighs. 'Sash, this isn't something you can keep secret. Once they suss we're missing, it'll be chaos back there.

They'll ring your parents. Sheddie'll ring my mum. They'll probably get the police . . .'

'The police?' I say, alarmed.

'Wouldn't you?' Jake asks. 'Two teens go missing from home of much-loved pop legend . . . we'll be front-page news if Matt has his way. He wanted a scoop, didn't he?'

I'm horrified. 'That can't happen,' I whisper. 'Can it?'

'Not if you tell people you're safe,' Jake says with a shrug. 'Best to do it now, before the film people turn up. And while you've still got a signal!'

'Can't you?'

'My phone's almost out of battery and I left in a hurry, so I don't have a charger,' Jake says. 'I'll text Sheddie and he can explain to everyone at Fox Hollow Hall . . . and tell my mum. You call home, let your family know you're safe. OK?'

'But I'll be home in a few hours anyway!' I protest.

'You might not be,' Jake reasons. 'We won't get to Barnstaple for a while . . . we can find the station and work out how to get to Millford from there. Have you got money?'

'Yeah, sure . . . about twenty-three pounds and some small change. How about you?'

'Not even a tenner after buying the bus tickets,' Jake says. 'Do me a favour . . . look up train times from Barnstaple to Millford, yeah?'

I do as he says and my heart sinks like a stone. A single ticket to Millford starts at £76, involves four changes and won't get me home until morning. I really, really haven't thought this through.

'What'll we do?' I wail. 'Where will we sleep? There's a six-hour wait for that last train, and I don't have anything like enough money for a ticket . . .'

'I'll think of something,' Jake says. 'Right now you need to call your family, tell them something's come up and you'll be home tomorrow. Or text at least. I'll text Sheddie. The time for keeping secrets is past, Sasha – you know that.'

I bite my lip. Jake's right . . . Trying to keep my troubles secret has backfired badly, and it won't be just me who pays the price.

There's silence for a moment while the two of us let the world know we're safe. I opt to text because it's easier to fake an upbeat tone, to make my early return seem normal and natural, a last-minute change of plans rather than a tearful escape with terrible consequences for the rest of the band.

A message from Mum pings back, telling me she's sorry things have been cut short but that she's missed me and will organize something special for tea. The fear that something is going wrong between my parents surfaces again, but, whatever's happening, I need my dad's quiet strength and my mum's hugs. I wonder how I will tell them the truth about how I'm feeling, what I've done. I know I'll have to find a way.

'Sheddie's going to tell Ked and Camille,' Jake reports. 'The OK Film team have arrived and everyone's a bit worried that we're missing, but Lexie and Marley are doing their best to present our ideas. Sheddie'll sort it out, explain – he's good in a crisis, stays calm.'

'Is he going to tell them I've left the band?'

'He'll do his best . . .'

Another tear slides down my cheek, cold and salty. You'd think there'd be no more left by now, but my traitorous body clearly has a few in reserve. I think about Sheddie trying to explain that I've gone home, that I don't want to be in the Lost & Found any more.

I'm a coward, I know. A braver person would have knocked on the kitchen door, gone in and faced Ked and

Camille. Instead, Jake's stepdad is left to clean up the mess for me.

Will Ked and Camille realize I overheard their conversation? Or will they think that my disappearance has saved them the job of firing me? I have no idea. I know my friends will be upset, but that will turn to anger when they understand that I've left them without a lead singer just when they were on the brink of being discovered.

All Ked's hard work to bring us down here, mentoring and recording us, inviting a top industry video crew to film us and a famous TV and radio personality to meet us . . . all of it was for nothing. The recording is nowhere near finished, and I don't see anyone making a video for a band with no lead singer.

I feel sick with shame. I've behaved like a spoiled toddler, smashing up the whole game just because it wasn't working out for me. But what else could I have done?

We're in a town now and finally bright lights shine outside the darkened windows as the bus lurches to a standstill. 'Barnstaple,' the driver calls. 'Everybody off!'

We stumble out into the rainy night.

*

We find the station easily enough, but we've missed the train to Exeter and we don't have a ticket anyway, so we huddle in a little cafe, sipping hot chocolate.

'There are options,' Jake tells me. 'We can travel without a ticket . . . it's a small station and there aren't any barriers. We can pretend the ticket machine was out of order.'

'But if we get caught, we'll still have to pay,' I argue.

'We could hide in the toilets if there's a ticket check,' Jake suggests. 'Or pretend to be asleep.'

'Or just pay as far as Exeter,' I say, because I am not a risk-taker or a lawbreaker. 'We might be able to afford that. But we'd still be miles and miles from Millford!'

'We could hitch a lift from there,' Jake offers.

'What! With a stranger?' I panic. 'No way! We'd end up murdered in a ditch! Are you mad?'

Jake shrugs. 'We could just stay here, try to sleep on the station platform, or at the bus station . . .'

'We'd freeze to death!'

'Picky, aren't you?' Jake teases. 'OK, so I'll make a few calls, sort a private jet to come and pick us up . . .'

The world shifts a little and I jump back to reality with the sting of something hot burning through my sleeve. The

mug I was cradling a moment ago lies on its side on the table top in a pool of hot chocolate, and Jake is mopping up the spill with a wad of serviettes.

'You OK?' he asks me. 'It wasn't too hot, was it?'

I pull the wet fabric away from my arm, but I know I'm not hurt, just embarrassed. Again.

'I look a mess,' I whisper. 'I am a mess . . . oh, Jake, what am I going to do?'

'You look fine,' he counters. 'You could be wearing an old potato sack with mud and ashes on your face, Sasha, and you'd still look beautiful to me . . . this will all work out, you'll see!'

I start to laugh, and Jake joins in. 'I have a plan,' he says. 'But you have to trust me, OK? We can't get you home tonight, but I know a place we can stay, some friends who'll help us. They're in Somerset and that's not far from here. My phone's died and I can't remember the number, but if you lend me your mobile I'll Google it . . .'

Jake scrolls through the internet. He must find what he's looking for, because he jabs in a number and then stands up and drifts to the back of the cafe to talk. I watch his face as the concerned frown melts away to be replaced by a

266

huge grin, and I am so glad to have him here with me that I feel myself filling up with a ridiculous, fizzing surge of happiness. My life is a mess – I've quit the band, possibly a split second before being fired; I've let down my friends and cost Britain's favourite pop legend a fortune in wasted time and money. I can't even manage to run away properly, but maybe none of this is the end of the world as long as I have Jake with me.

I watch him talking, noticing the way his sandy-blond hair sticks up in random directions, like a small tornado just passed through. I notice how his eyes, a dark blue-grey, spark and shine as he winks at me across the half-empty cafe. Jake is cute and kind and clever, and I would trust him with pretty much anything.

He's back, handing me the phone and grabbing his jacket.

'OK . . . we have to head back to the bus station,' he tells me. 'There's a bus to a place called Lynton leaving in ten minutes, and we need to be on it . . . or we really are stuck here for the night! Ready?'

We run through the streets, hand in hand, splashing through puddles. We make the bus with a minute to spare,

and moments later we're rattling through the darkened lanes heading to who-knows-where.

'Why are you helping me, Jake?' I ask as we huddle together, catching our breath. 'You've given up your chance to be involved in the video, even though a lot of it was your idea. You didn't have to follow me . . . why did you?'

'I wanted to,' he said simply. 'It wouldn't have been any fun without you around. Besides . . . you weren't thinking straight, you hadn't planned this. I figured you could use some help.'

'And you're an expert in running away,' I state. 'When you did it – what made you run? I can't imagine anything rattling you enough to do something like that.'

Jake laughs. 'Ha – last summer I was a walking disaster,' he tells me. 'I was upset because Mum wanted to move us to Millford to live with this bloke she'd just met – Sheddie. I didn't like the idea of it, and then I made an epically stupid mistake and just about wrecked the flat we were living in. I thought I'd lost Mum her job too, and I couldn't see any way out . . .'

'So you ran?'

'I ran,' he confirms. 'I'd just found out I had four half-sisters who lived in Somerset . . . I'd never met my dad, but

they were his kids, and one of them had been writing to me. I thought I'd go and find them, find out more about my dad . . .'

'And?' I press.

'And it turned out he was living in Australia,' Jake explains. 'When I finally got to talk to him, he was just as big a loser as my mum had said he was. Which was kind of a let-down. But my half-sisters – they were cool. Honey's the eldest, and then there's the twins – Skye's vintage mad and Summer's a dancer. Coco's my age – she's a bit of an eco warrior. Their mum married again, a bloke called Paddy, so there's a stepsister too, Cherry. Anyway, that's where we're going now!'

I blink. 'To see your sisters?'

Jake shrugs. 'It's where I always go when I run away,' he quips. 'Don't worry, you'll like them!'

Sasha, where are you? The film crew are here and Ked and Camille are asking where you and Jake are – we're trying to stall for time, but it's not easy. Hurry up! Romy x

Please tell me where you are. Ked sent the film crew home and he's been in a huddle with the other adults for ages now. Something's up. Please answer! Romy x

Whatever's happened, Sash, please come back. We're all so worried! Lexie x

Please let us know you're OK! Happi x

You've really blown it now. Ked's raging, and Marley will never forgive you. But hey, I got some great photos of your meltdown. M

25

Tanglewood

I must have slept, because I wake as the bus rumbles to a halt, with Jake's arm round me, my head on his shoulder.

'I can see the van,' Jake says as he swings my case down the steps and on to the pavement, and I follow his gaze through the darkness towards a strangely shaped maroon-and-cream-painted van that seems to be advertising some kind of chocolate. The doors slide open and a man and a girl jump out. Jake hugs each of them in turn.

'This is Sasha,' he tells them. 'My friend from the band. Sasha, this is Paddy and my half-sister Coco!'

Coco looks about the same age as Jake and me, with fair hair in a pixie cut, a Greenpeace T-shirt and the biggest grin I've ever seen.

'Hello,' I say shyly. 'Thank you for rescuing us!'

'No worries,' Paddy says. 'Any friend of Cookie's and all that! You're soaked . . . let's see if we can warm you up a bit.'

We all squash into the van while Paddy starts the engine and turns the heater up, and everyone is talking, catching up on news as I try to gather my thoughts and tune in.

'The van's been brilliant,' Paddy is saying. 'It's French, a vintage Citroën – the side opens so we can use it for pop-up chocolate events and festivals as well as deliveries. Always draws a crowd! It's not fast, but it should have us home in half an hour, even in this downpour, and Charlotte's making soup . . .'

'Is everyone home?' Jake asks.

'No,' Coco says. 'Honey, Cherry and Shay have gone up to London, so just me and the twins. It's half-term, so at least Summer's home! You should have warned us – we could have gathered the clans . . . we thought you were at that pop star's place being groomed for stardom!'

'Change of plan,' Jake says. 'And besides, I was just the tech guy!'

'Our favourite tech guy,' Paddy says easily. 'And now we get to see you and meet Sasha, so it's win–win, right? Apart from getting yourselves stranded, of course. You did the right thing calling us – two kids wandering around the countryside at night with no money . . . bad idea.'

'We know,' Jake says. 'I'm sorry!'

The chat goes on around me as I dream and gaze out into the darkness, and then at last the van turns off the road and bumps along past trees strung with fairy lights and lanterns. It feels like we've stepped out of the real world for a moment into somewhere different, somewhere magical.

The van halts in front of a big Victorian house with an actual turret on one corner.

'Welcome to Tanglewood,' Paddy says as we get out, and the door bursts open, new people spilling out to greet us.

A woman with blonde hair bundled into a messy updo – Paddy's wife, Charlotte – and the twins, Skye and Summer, welcome us with hugs and chatter, while a bouncy dog runs around at our feet. I'm almost sure I see a lone sheep

peering at me from behind one of the outbuildings, but decide I must be hallucinating.

'I made soup,' Charlotte is saying. 'Tomato . . . is that OK? And there's freshly baked soda bread and cake leftover from teatime.'

'Amazing,' Jake says. 'Thank you!'

'What were you doing stranded in the Devonshire countryside at this time of night? In the rain too?' asks the twin in leggings and an outsize pink fluffy jumper. Her blonde plaits are pinned up round her head, ballerina style – she must be the dancer, Summer.

'You haven't run away again, have you?' the other twin asks. This one seems to be wearing a dress that looks like it's made from a jumble-sale curtain printed with pots and pans, but nobody seems to think this is unusual. Skye, the twin obsessed with vintage and history. 'I thought things were working out for you, Jake. Band on the way to fame and fortune, roadie to the stars and all that. What happened?'

'My fault,' I say. 'I'm supposed to be the band's lead singer, but I've been really unhappy the last few months. I have some weird kind of health issue. Things weren't working out. I had to get away, and Jake came with me because . . . well, because I had no clue what I was doing on my own.'

'Because I care about you,' he says, his cheeks suddenly pink, and a little glow of happiness lights up inside me, in spite of all the chaos I've created. Jake cares.

'Right,' Charlotte says. 'I take it you've let people know where you are? We won't have the police landing on us?'

'No, everyone knows we're safe,' Jake says.

Charlotte nods. 'Well, let's get you fed first . . . and then you can tell us all about it, and we'll see what can be done.'

I manage half a bowl of soup – the lush, rich kind that definitely hasn't come out of a tin.

'So,' Coco says. 'Why has the lead singer of the Lost & Found band run away just when they're on the edge of stardom? Jake told us you were in Devon – recording with Ked Wilder. That's the chance of a lifetime for anyone interested in a music career, right? What went wrong?'

I sigh. How to make them understand?

'I overheard a conversation I shouldn't have,' I say softly. 'Ked and Camille – she's the voice coach – were talking about me, about how I wasn't cut out to front a band. I heard every word and it was all true. I'm the weak link – the one who can't quite deliver on star quality.'

Jake looks stricken. 'That's not true, Sasha,' he says. 'You're amazing – you have a beautiful voice –'

'I'm a liability,' I interrupt. 'I've been having these weird blanking-out episodes, blackouts . . . well, for ages now. They scare me, so I ignore them . . . pretend they're not happening. Jake wants me to see a doctor, but I'm scared of what they might say. What if it's something serious?'

'What if it isn't?' Charlotte replies, eyes wide. 'You can't just ignore something like that! It could be easily fixable.'

I shake my head. 'Not everything is,' I say. 'I've tried to hide it from the band, but I can't, not any more. People have started to notice, and it's getting worse. And it's not just that . . . the truth is, I don't want to be in the Lost & Found anyway. Fronting a band isn't my dream – it feels more like a nightmare!'

'But . . . why didn't you tell them?' Skye asks, baffled.

'I didn't realize what I was getting into at first. It was fun to start with, and then suddenly everything got serious. The festival, the radio, playing live – I was out of my depth, but I didn't know how to say so. Nobody had a clue – not my

friends, not even my parents. It took me a while to work it out – I thought it was just the usual butterflies before a performance, but it's much more than that. I can't do this, don't want to do this. But how could I say so without ruining things for everyone? I've been lying awake at night worrying about it for weeks and weeks!'

'Oh, Sasha!' Skye says.

'Once Ked invited us to Devon, I had no chance of coming clean,' I plough on. 'Marley made it clear that this is our big chance – can you imagine his reaction if I'd said I wasn't coming? If I'd said I was quitting the band? He'd never have forgiven me. I went along with it, hoping I could carry it off and that maybe I'd learn to love it like the others seem to . . . but that's not what's happened.'

I dab at my eyes with a soggy tissue. I hate a whole bunch of strangers seeing my gritty red eyes and blotchy face almost as much as I hate them seeing the mess that I am inside.

'I love singing,' I confess. 'But performing in front of people? Hate it. I can't eat, I feel sick, I can't breathe properly . . . it takes every bit of my strength and courage to make myself do it. Everyone says it gets easier with time, but it doesn't for me . . . I've been in knots every day, trying so hard because I didn't want to let everyone down. I know they were working out how to tell me I wasn't up to scratch . . . I've just saved them the trouble.'

'You don't know that,' Jake argues.

'I do,' I say. 'It's taken me a while to suss that I can't keep pretending to be someone I'm not, but I got there in the end.'

I notice Summer studying me carefully. 'I think you're brave,' she says quietly. 'Not everyone is so honest with themselves about what they can and can't do, and not everyone has the guts to admit it. You figured out that you didn't want this, and you had the courage to say so . . . I wish I'd been that sussed. It took me a while.'

'Summer wanted to be a principal dancer,' Coco chips in. 'But she hated the pressure. She's training to be a dance teacher now. She still gets to do the thing she loves, only with a lot less stress.'

Summer smiles at me and I see the sadness behind her smile. I know that she understands and that gives me strength.

'You really don't want to be in the Lost & Found?' Jake puzzles.

'I really, really don't. Not as the lead singer anyway.'

'So what is your dream then?' Coco wants to know.

'My dream?' I consider. 'Something more behind the scenes, like Jake – I'd love to be a make-up artist, work in TV or film maybe . . .'

Skye's face lights up. 'I want to study costume design – I've been researching uni courses,' she tells me. 'There are loads of courses in make-up for film and TV, or for fashion and media, special effects even . . . it's definitely possible!'

'Most things are possible,' Charlotte says, clearing away the soup dishes. 'We can talk about this again tomorrow, put you in touch with some people perhaps. They shot a film at Kitnor a couple of years ago, and we got quite friendly with the producer and the crew. And last year we were in a documentary about our chocolate business. We might have some contacts who could give you work experience.'

I nod, hopeful now. Ria and Fitz offered the same thing . . . There is a different path if I'm brave enough to follow it.

'We're happy to book you both a train ticket home,' Paddy offers. 'Unless you want Sheddie to drive you, of course, or Sasha's parents want to come and fetch you . . .'

Jake shrugs. 'Maybe Sheddie can drive, or maybe we'll take the tickets. If we do, we'll pay you back!'

'Obviously,' I say. 'We're really grateful for all your help!'

'You're welcome,' Charlotte says, cutting slices of fudge cake. 'I know you're upset, of course you are, but Summer's right – you've been brave, really.'

I sigh. 'It's such a mess, though. I wish I'd had the courage to say something sooner, then I wouldn't have dropped everyone in it quite so badly. I've wrecked it for everyone!'

Coco waves her spoon at me. 'Don't be a drama queen about it,' she says. 'OK, you've quit – that's not going to make you popular with some of the band. But don't kid yourself – they'll get a new lead singer. From what Jake's told us, they're talented and ambitious. They're not going to give up just because you've dropped out, are they?'

'You think?' I ask, hope unfurling inside me.

'I know,' Coco says.

Paddy makes hot chocolate and we sit round the big scrubbed-pine kitchen table for another hour or so, Skye talking about her new A levels, Summer about her work as trainee teacher at a residential ballet school, Coco about the campaigns she's running to make her school a

plastic-free zone and one that only uses sustainable palm oil. 'We've raised three hundred pounds to save the orang-utans,' she tells me. 'I wrote to the paper about it!'

The more I get to know them, the more I like Jake's half-sisters. They're sparky and cool and very kind, and I wonder how Jake's dad could have betrayed Charlotte and her girls for a brief affair with Jake's mum. According to Jake, he then abandoned everyone and moved to Australia, and Jake says they're better off without him because Charlotte's got Paddy now, as well as a thriving artisan chocolate business, and Jake's mum has Sheddie. Everyone's happy.

I think about my parents, working through their troubles and coming out the other side . . . perhaps. Surely if they've weathered the storms once, they can do it again? Tonight is Tuesday, when Mum works until seven and Dad cooks his signature sausage and mash dinner, served with glasses of Irn-Bru . . . I wish I'd been there to share it.

I'm not sure how I got to the point where I felt I had to hide my feelings from my parents, pretend to be something I'm not. It seems crazy right now, because I know without a doubt that even if they stop loving each other they will

always love me, whether I am the lead singer of a famous band or not.

'Families come in all shapes and sizes,' Jake tells me, grinning. 'Mine's a real jigsaw, but I wouldn't be without them!'

Later Charlotte shows me to the turret bedroom that belongs to Honey, her eldest daughter, who is currently in London. 'Sleep well,' she says. 'Things will look brighter in the morning!'

I plug my mobile in to charge, slip between the crisp, cool sheets and fall into a dreamless sleep.

By morning the rain has stopped and the smell of cooked breakfast drifts through the house. I still feel tired, as well as a little shivery and achy, but I'm thrilled to be waking up in an actual turret. Coco sticks her head round the bedroom door to tell me the sausages are veggie ones, because going meat-free is better for the planet, and can I hurry up and get dressed because she wants to show me something.

I shower and dress and do my make-up as fast as I can, and head downstairs in perfect time for veggie sausages,

I kick off my shoes, peel off my socks and walk into the water. It's ice-cold, the kind of cold that makes you cry out, but still, I plunge my hands in. What do I wish for? A second chance, a chance to be true to myself, to get things right.

By the time we start back up the rickety steps my teeth are chattering, and I'm somehow shivery and too hot both at the same time. My head feels fuzzy and I zone out halfway up, but when I come back to myself Jake has an arm round my waist, holding me safe.

'OK?' he checks.

'I don't know,' I admit. 'I feel a bit weird . . . sort of achy and hot and cold. Maybe it's because of getting soaked in the storm last night.'

'Maybe,' Jake says, frowning.

As we walk back through the trees and across the grass to the house, I'm aware of Coco chatting on, talking about deforestation and whether or not Paddy and Charlotte will be putting solar panels on the roof of the chocolate workshop, but I can't seem to follow it.

My body seems slow and heavy. As I step off the grass and on to the gravel driveway, I hear the sound of a car

285

engine and turn to see a familiar white van chugging up towards the house. Sheddie.

I turn to Jake, dismayed. 'I don't understand . . . what's he doing here?'

'I don't know,' Jake says. 'Maybe Paddy and Charlotte called his mobile. Maybe . . . I don't know!'

The van stops at an angle and three figures get out – Sheddie grinning, Romy, her face filled with relief, waving, and Matt, lips twisted into a mean, smirky smile, camera in hand.

'Found you!' he says. 'Is it true you've quit the band, Sasha?'

The world tilts and blurs. My knees give way and I'm falling, my cheek and palms stinging as they hit the gravel. Darkness bleeds into the edges of my vision like spilled ink, and everything goes black.

SashaSometimes

325 likes

SashaSometimes Change of plan . . .

littlejen First like!

LexiiieLooks Where are you? Please get in touch!

HappiDaze Sasha please call! So worried!

OllieK What's up?

PetraB Has something happened?

Yorkie_Joe Lexie and Happi are from the band – something's happened to Sasha!

26

After

There are so many ways to disappear. You can hide behind
a curtain and pretend it's a game, or vanish into your own
mind a dozen times a day and tell yourself you're travelling
through time or experimenting with astrophysics. You can
run away into the night because you don't have the guts to
tell your friends you're not the person they thought you
were, or you can get ill and let a fever swallow you up,
drifting in and out of it for days.

I'd never had flu before, the kind that has you spiking a
temperature one minute and shivering the next, the kind that
makes your bones ache and turns your throat to sandpaper.
It wasn't nice, but I was sure it wasn't the kind of thing you

had to be in hospital for. I didn't understand why I was stuck on a trolley in a room where the lights were too bright, where doctors in white coats asked strange questions and nurses kept a chart of my pulse, my blood pressure, my temperature.

I didn't understand why Jake and Romy and Sheddie were sitting by my trolley bed looking scared, or why Mum and Dad were suddenly there, hugging me through the thin hospital blanket and holding my hand as the doctors ran a test that involved electrodes and wires being stuck all over my scalp.

'Just leave her!' my mum sobbed halfway through, when a barrage of bright, pulsing strobe lights flashed right into my eyes. 'This is cruel! Please stop!'

Maybe it was just a bad dream, because nobody told me what the outcome was. In the end, we were allowed to go and I slept most of the way home to Millford in the back of Dad's car, a blanket tucked round me.

I stayed in bed for three days, achy and feverish, my mind fuzzy and drifting.

On the fourth day I am much better. It's Saturday and Mum is back at work. Dad too, because he has a couple of

jobs to finish that had overrun because of his emergency dash south to fetch me. I shower and wash my hair and change into clean leggings and a slouchy top. I eat some soup at a kitchen table dominated by a huge bouquet of white roses sent by Ked. There's a basket of fruit from Sheddie and Jake too, a new library book by my favourite teen author dropped off by Romy and a fancy box of artisan chocolate truffles from Charlotte and Paddy at Tanglewood.

There's a pile of unopened post on the kitchen counter, including a padded envelope addressed to me that may or may not contain the mobile I left at Tanglewood. I'm not exactly in a hurry to see it, or to read the messages and texts it holds, but I open the padded envelope anyway and plug the phone and charger into the wall.

Sifting through the post, I find a get-well card from the band, hand-drawn by Sami and featuring loads of tiny sketches of our time in Devon. Everyone has signed it and scribbled little messages – maybe they're not as mad at me as I think?

The rest of the post is boring brown-envelope stuff – bills and circulars, a letter from the hospital, a rolled-up

newspaper tied with string and seemingly hand-delivered. It looks like a copy of today's *Daily Scoop*, one of the trashier tabloids, not a paper we usually get. Boring.

I think of Romy, of Marley and Lexie, of Sami, Happi, Bex, Lee, George and Dylan . . . and Jake, of course. I owe them an apology, an explanation. I need to know if we can still be friends.

I take a deep breath and pick up my phone. There are hundreds of texts, messages and missed calls, dating from Tuesday night right up to now . . . Saturday. My hand shakes as I click on the latest ones, but I force myself to read.

> Don't forget we're having a
> Halloween party at the old
> railway carriage. Meeting
> midday. See you there –
> counting on you to make me
> look scary! Lee x

> Hope you're feeling better. Why
> aren't you answering your

291

messages? Did you get the
library book? Romy x

Are you coming to the
Halloween thing? Don't be late!
We have cake! If you're not well
enough, let us know and we'll
come to you. Miss you loads.
Lexie xox

I know you're ill but call me
when you can, Sasha. We can
work this out. Seriously, we
can't do without you. Marley x

Your mum and dad said you're
not well enough to see me, but
I'll keep calling and messaging
until you're better – just say the
word and I'll be round with my
wheelbarrow. Miss you millions.
Jake x

My friends aren't mad at me . . . they're just worried! Relief floods through me. And then I see a message from Matt.

Fame at last. Page five of today's
Daily Scoop – hope you like it!
All publicity is good publicity,
right? M

I blink. The *Daily Scoop*? I glance at the rolled-up newspaper on the kitchen counter, untie the string and flick through to page five with shaking hands. There – underneath a piece about a middle-aged soap star seen out clubbing with a man fifteen years her junior – are two pictures of me.

A full-colour picture of me with mascara running down my face in rivulets, looking upset and angry. And another of me lying on the gravel, face cut, completely out of it, a thin trail of spittle sliding out of my mouth and down my cheek.

My heart is thumping and I feel cold all over, and this time it has nothing to do with the flu. My fingers shake as I read the headline: 'Wilder's Teen Band Shatters – Singer's Dark Secret Derails A Promising Future'.

'No. Way . . .' I whisper, but my voice has withered to a sad, sick croak, and I'm battling nausea as I force myself to read on.

Rumours of drink, drugs or serious illness were rife this week as the teen singer of up-and-coming band the Lost & Found, tipped for the top by pop legend Ked Wilder, quit the band and subsequently collapsed not far from the star's Devon home. A source close to the band told us that fourteen-year-old Sasha Kaminski had been struggling with the pressure as the band recorded their first single at the private studios of their famous mentor.

'She didn't feel she belonged in the band,' our source revealed. 'She wasn't coping. I don't know if the collapse was down to drink, drugs or illness, but I do know that it was never a good idea for ten vulnerable young teens to stay unsupervised with an ageing pop star for a week. Wilder pushed them way too hard.'

There's a smaller picture of the whole band together and a decades-old stock photo of Ked looking rakish and holding a bottle of beer.

I take in a ragged breath. My whole body is shaking with the injustice of it all, the lies. Matt Brennan took these photos. He almost certainly posted a copy of the *Scoop* through our door, making sure I'd see it. He has blackened my name, betrayed my friends, thrown Ked's kindness back in his face. I blink away tears. If my running away hasn't hurt the Lost & Found enough, this will finish the job for sure.

A rush of anger pushes my self-pity aside. In my bedroom I brush my hair till it shines, lean into the mirror to paint perfect cat's-eye flicks, haul out the little suitcase of make-up and face paints. I promised to see my friends at Halloween . . . this time I will not let them down.

My cheek and hands are still grazed and sore from falling on the gravel at Tanglewood. I could take a moment to camouflage the damage, but the idea seems crazy – I'll wear my pain with pride.

I grab my jacket, pick up the suitcase and head for Greystones. It's not a long walk, but I'm still weak after the flu and I need every bit of courage and strength I have to get there. The moment I see the old railway carriage, my heart aches for everything I'm losing, but I walk right up to it and knock on the door.

There's no reply. No sound of music or voices, no sound of life at all. Did they cancel the party? I turn the handle and step inside, and a wisp of fake cobweb brushes against my face. The place is decorated for Halloween with leering paper skeletons and hanging spiders . . . but it's deserted.

Disappointed and weary, I sit down for a moment. The ghosts of all the good times we've had in this space seem to whirl around me, and I blink back tears.

And then I hear the sound of voices and laughter, and I run to the doorway and see the band coming across the grass, dressed in bizarre Halloween costumes and carrying instruments.

'Sasha!' Marley yells. 'You're here!'

Jake, wearing devil horns and carrying a Halloween lantern made from a pumpkin, legs it up the railway carriage steps, picks me up and whirls me round.

'Trick or treat?' he asks, grinning. 'We've just been to your house, but you weren't in!'

'I'm here,' I tell him. 'I've missed you!'

'I've missed you too,' Jake answers, and then Marley, terrifying in a skeleton onesie and brandishing his guitar, elbows him aside and pulls me into a hug.

296

He turns to the others. 'Ready?' he demands. 'Go!'

The rest of the band form a group round the door of the old railway carriage and Marley leaps down to join them as they launch into a wild open-air rendition of an old sixties song called 'I Only Want to Be With You'. Without a lead singer, their vocals are ever so slightly dodgy.

It's quite surreal to watch Dracula, Frankenstein and a whole posse of ghosts, zombies and werewolves bopping about in the flower beds and playing trumpet, violin and tomtom drums. It's possible that I'm hallucinating, of course, but when the song is over and they bound up the steps to catch me in a big, messy group hug, I have to accept it's real.

'Your face!' Marley says, wincing. 'Looks sore!'

'I had an argument with some gravel,' I quip.

'You haven't been answering our texts and calls,' he says. 'When you didn't turn up earlier, we thought you'd vanished off the face of the earth – so we went to find you. We had to get your attention somehow. We're all in agreement, Sash – we don't want another lead singer. We only want you! Like the song says!'

'I've quit,' I tell him. 'I should have done it a while ago. I never planned to mess up your big chance for fame . . . I'm so sorry! I haven't been answering your messages because I left my phone at Tanglewood . . . just got it back today. I know you must be mad at me. I've been an idiot!'

'Yes, but you're our idiot,' Marley says. 'Don't worry, we'll sort this out!'

Not everything can be sorted out, but I'm not sure Marley's seeing that just yet.

I bite my lip, pulling the rolled-up newspaper from my shoulder bag. 'There's something else . . . something terrible. Matt Brennan . . .'

'You saw it then?' Bex says. 'Horrible, right? What a loser!'

'But . . . it's all lies!' I manage to say. 'There were no drink or drugs involved! I just fainted! And we were supervised the whole time . . . None of this is true! Poor Ked!'

'There's a whole section on his decadent lifestyle and the monogrammed towels in his bathroom,' Marley retorts. 'Matt must have been snooping around Ked's private apartment. I've spoken to Ked, and he's not too worried . . .

298

says he's had worse things written about him. He's more upset about you, Sasha, and how you're feeling.'

'I feel . . . awful,' I grate out. 'Betrayed. Matt was supposed to be our friend – how could he do this?'

Jake raises an eyebrow. 'Ambition,' he says starkly. 'Money too, I bet. Poisonous little skunk . . . wait till I get my hands on him!'

'What do we do now?' I ask, anger bubbling to the surface again. 'Get in touch with the paper, put our side of the story? We can't let him get away with it!'

Marley shakes his head. 'Ked reckons it's best to ignore it. Fighting back would just fan the flames. So we made the national newspapers . . . well, so what? It's rubbish. The band hasn't shattered and no bright futures have been derailed. We carry on just the same as before.'

'Without me,' I remind him.

Marley rolls his eyes. 'Yeah, about that,' he says. 'We don't want you to go over some silly misunderstanding, Sasha. Ked feels awful – he and Camille were just worried, and talking about how to support you. We've all been texting and calling non-stop, and when you didn't answer we had the idea of serenading you with that song!'

'We miss you,' Lexie says simply.

'And we brought cake,' Happi adds, prising the lid off a tin of cupcakes iced to look like spiders and passing it round.

Lee unwraps a length of bloodstained bandage from his head in order to attack his cupcake more efficiently. 'We need you, Sasha,' he says between mouthfuls. 'Don't go!'

I shake my head. 'I don't belong in the Lost & Found,' I say sadly. 'Ked and Camille were right – I'm not cut out for it!'

Marley rakes a hand through his hair. 'No, no, no! You are! You look great – you have the voice of an angel . . . and besides, Ked doesn't call the shots here. We do! We know you're not well, but we can work round that. It can be treated, obviously. It's not a problem.'

'It was only flu,' I point out. 'I'll be fine in a couple of days!'

My friends exchange glances, frowning, and I feel I'm missing something, that they know something I don't.

'Shut up, Marley,' Jake says, glaring. 'Leave it. OK?'

Marley shrugs. 'Whatever,' he says. 'Just stick with us, Sasha. We can make this work, I promise!'

A rush of gratitude fills me, sweeter even than the Halloween cupcakes, but I have to be honest.

'I've quit,' I repeat. 'It's just . . . it's not my dream, Marley. Not like it is for you guys. My heart isn't in it and I don't want to hold you back.'

Marley looks defeated. 'You weren't holding us back,' he says. 'If you want to quit, OK, but don't be too hasty. If you change your mind . . . band practice is at five o'clock tomorrow. Think about it, Sasha, please?'

'It won't be the same without you,' Romy says. 'We'll miss you like mad, but no hard feelings . . . except for that lowlife Matt, obviously.'

Lexie is nodding. 'We wish you well, whatever you decide. We'll still see you all the time at school anyway, and maybe . . . could you be the band stylist or something?'

'Starting from now,' I say, opening my make-up case. 'I promised, didn't I? I have face paint, I have fake blood, I have willing victims . . .'

'Yesss!' Dylan grins.

Lexie puts a Halloween-themed playlist on the sound system, Happi pours mugs of blood-coloured fruit punch and George grabs first turn in the hot seat, asking if I can make him look like Dracula.

I spread page five of the *Daily Scoop* across the counter-top and use it to mix my paints.

 **SashaSometimes**

376 likes

SashaSometimes I'll be deactivating this account in a day or two. I've stepped down from the band as lead singer, although I'll still be working with them on and off and of course we're all still friends. Thanks for the follows and the likes – they meant a lot. Love ya. Xxx
#NoMoreBandLife #Lost&Found #Quitting #NoMakeUpSelfie #DigitalDetox #RealMe #NobodysPerfect

Comments for this post have been disabled.

27

Secrets

Jake walks me home, only attracting a few stares with his devil horns and newly painted face.

'OK?' he asks.

I laugh. 'Just great,' I say. 'Today's news is tomorrow's garbage, right?'

'You said it. And today's ace reporter is tomorrow's has-been. Matt's a loser, end of story.'

I nod, but there's something still bothering me, something that doesn't feel quite right. That moment when my friends looked at each other, as if they knew something I didn't . . .

'Jake . . . what is it you're not telling me?' I ask. 'What is it you told Marley not to say, just before?'

He looks awkward. 'Your mum hasn't spoken to you?' he says. 'About what happened that morning when you fell?'

'I've been out of it these last few days,' I say, putting a hand to the gravel burns on my cheek. 'Sleeping most of the time. I know what happened, though. I fainted. Typical me – I had to fall down on gravel and not the grass.'

Jake's eyes darken. He opens his mouth to speak and then closes it again, uncertain. 'You really don't remember?'

Fear coils like a snake in my belly.

'Talk to your parents, Sash,' he says. 'Ask them, OK?'

He kisses me and plants the red devil horns on my head as a parting gift.

Mum makes pasta for tea, and Dad pours orange juice into fancy wine glasses so we can toast the fact that I'm getting better.

'I saw Jake today,' I tell them casually. 'He told me to ask you what happened when I fainted. What did he mean?'

Dad frowns and Mum's cheeks burn pink.

'It wasn't a faint,' she tells me quietly. 'When you fell over. It was more a kind of seizure. Like a fit. A convulsion.'

'A . . . seizure?' I echo. 'What? What d'you mean?'

'Well, we weren't there, obviously, but it scared your friends,' she continues. 'You went stiff and jerky, and your eyes rolled back in your head. They didn't know what to do, but apparently Charlotte came running out, and she'd had first-aid training so she knew what it was. She put a scarf under your head to stop the gravel cutting you, and when the seizure was over she rolled you on your side and called an ambulance.'

'I had a seizure?' I repeat, unable to take this in. '*A seizure?*'

I remember the weird test at the hospital, the one where they wired me up to a machine and flashed lights in my face. The doctors took a trace of what was happening in my brain.

According to Mum, it was a test to check for epilepsy.

I roll the word around in my head, but it feels so clumsy, so frightening. No wonder I could never be perfect with something like that hidden beneath the surface.

'Jake told us about the blackout moments you've been having,' Dad says gently. 'We'd noticed that a couple of times, but we didn't know what it was – we thought you were dreaming, zoning out. Turns out those blackout moments are a form of epilepsy. Absence seizures, they're called. It's like your brain has some kind of short circuit and just cuts out . . . something like that. The hospital has referred you for an appointment with a specialist in Millford so they can start you on medication and get things under control.'

I can't make sense of any of this. 'So they can treat it?' I check. 'This . . . absence thing?'

'They definitely can,' Mum says. 'We've been reading up about it. Now they know what's wrong, they can give you meds to stop it happening.'

I want to laugh out loud. It's not funny, of course, but the relief is huge . . . the black-hole moments are a real thing and they can be treated.

'I thought it was anxiety,' I say. 'Worry about being in the band, being the lead singer. I looked it up on the internet!'

'The internet?' Dad huffs. 'Full of rubbish! You love being in the band!'

I sigh. 'I don't actually,' I admit. 'I haven't for ages. I get sick with nerves every time I have to perform, and sick with worry that I'm not good enough. That's why I ran away from Fox Hollow Hall – I just couldn't do it any more!'

Dad looks stricken. 'But why didn't you say? We were so proud of you! I don't understand!'

'Why didn't you just tell us, Sasha?' Mum asks. 'About the blackouts, and how you really felt?'

I shake my head. 'I wanted to,' I explain. 'I really did, but I was scared you'd be disappointed in me. You think I'm some kind of perfect daughter – I've tried so very hard to be – but I'm really, really not. I'm a mess!'

'You're not a mess!' Mum scolds. 'And you don't have to be perfect, Sasha – we're not, so why should you be? We love you no matter what.'

Tears mist my eyes, and first Mum hugs me tight, then Dad.

'You always were a sensitive child,' Mum says. 'Wanting things to be perfect – but life's not like that. You've always pushed yourself too hard. That's why I was so happy you'd joined the Lost & Found – you had friends, you were having fun! That was all we ever cared about.'

There are so many things I got wrong, it seems. I put myself under so much pressure that things were bound to crack in the end . . . and I'm almost glad they have, because it means I don't have to hide any more, don't have to pretend to be someone I'm not.

'When we see the doctor . . . can I ask about anxiety too?' I say. 'Because I'd like things to be different and I'm not sure I can change on my own. They'd take it seriously, right?'

'Of course they would,' Mum says. 'Oh, Sash – if you'd just told us all this before!'

'I almost did,' I confess. 'Just before we went away. It was that day I came in and you were arguing, and then Dad went out . . . I got scared. I thought you were fighting again. You know . . . like when I was little!'

I look from Mum to Dad, waiting for them to laugh, to push away my fears, but their faces are serious. 'Oh, Sasha,' Dad says. 'I'm sorry! We didn't think. We didn't know . . .'

The ground slides away from under my feet all over again.

'What is it?' I demand. 'What's wrong? Is it work? Money? Have you . . . are you –'

Mum holds up a hand. 'It's OK, love,' she says. 'We're fine. I promise. You're right, though – things have been pretty stressful these last few months. We didn't want to worry you . . .'

'I was worried,' I say. 'I'm worried now! What's wrong?'

Dad reaches out across the table, takes my hand. 'You won't really remember, Sasha, but when you were little we did go through a bad patch. Your mum lost a baby and was told she probably couldn't have any more, and she got very sad and low afterwards. I got angry – it seemed so unfair. I drank too much and we argued a lot, but we got through it.'

'I do remember,' I tell him. 'I do.'

Dad nods. 'Well, the thing is . . . the doctors were wrong, Sasha. They were wrong! Your mum's having a baby!'

My scrambled head can't make sense of the news. 'Wh-what?' I stutter. 'How? Are you sure? Is everything OK?'

Mum is laughing. 'We're very sure,' she says. 'And yes, everything's fine – I'm twenty weeks in and I had a second scan while you were away, just to be sure. The doctors think I'm past the danger point now. We've both been working extra shifts to save some money for the baby, and that day you caught us arguing – well, your dad was worried, he thought I was doing too much. That's all it was. You're going to have a little sister, Sash!'

Mum puts her arms round me and holds me close, and this time I can feel the little bump of her tummy pressing against me. My little sister. Tears are rolling down my cheeks as if they'll never stop, but I've never been so happy in my life.

We have a whole lot more talking to do, of course. We talk about the epilepsy, about the newspaper article, about me quitting the band. It turns out that none of it is the end of the world. The epilepsy can be controlled, my parents say, and there's a chance I will grow out of it in time. Nobody takes any notice of the *Daily Scoop*, Dad reckons, but he's furious the paper printed my name and photos and is going to demand an apology. He's also going to talk to Mr Simpson, the school principal. 'Matt Brennan will find he's in a lot of trouble,' Dad says. 'And so will the *Daily Scoop* . . . you're a minor, for goodness' sake! They're really out of order!'

Mum and Dad are fine about me leaving the band, although they tell me not to make any rash decisions, do anything I might regret. Whatever I decide, they're proud of me. I wonder why I ever thought it would be so hard to tell them the truth, or why I thought I had to be perfect for them to love me. Funny how you can get things so wrong.

On Sunday I find myself thinking a lot about Marley's offer to come to band practice. Maybe he's right? Maybe with meds and a bit more confidence I could hang on? Or maybe not.

As the clock creeps closer to five, I pull on my coat, tell Mum and Dad I'm going out, and walk over to Greystones. The street is wide and sweeping, carpeted with leaves from the many big trees that edge the park. I sit down on a low wall across the road from the Greystones gateway, and the darkness keeps me hidden as my friends arrive for band practice.

First I see Marley and Dylan turning into the gateway, then Happi, Bex and Lexie walking together and Sami in a new winter jacket so different from the tattered overcoat he used to wear. Lee and George and Romy are wrapped in various hats and scarves, hurrying so as not to be late.

Not one of them sees me hiding in the shadows. I am the invisible girl.

I imagine the old railway carriage lit up in the darkness, the heaters going full blast. I imagine Happi and Lexie making hot chocolate in the little galley kitchen, handing round chocolate chip cookies and listening to Marley outline some kind of plan for the future.

What would happen if I walked in there now and told them I'd changed my mind? They'd welcome me back with open arms, I know.

A figure appears on the driveway, a skinny boy with wind-tunnel hair and a lopsided smile. Jake comes out on to the pavement, scans up and down the street and finally spots me. He walks over, grinning, pulling himself up on to the wall beside me.

'Not coming in then?' he asks, nudging me gently. 'Sure?'

'Sure,' I tell him. 'I just . . . wanted to say goodbye, really. I feel so sad, Jake . . . they will find another singer, won't they?'

'Definitely,' he promises. 'Won't be a patch on you, though!'

He puts an arm round me and pulls me close, and I rest my head on his shoulder, smiling in the darkness.

A black cab turns into the street and pulls to a halt beside the gates. A girl gets out, a teenage girl with long red hair and what looks like a wickerwork cat basket in one hand. She pays the driver and I see her clearly for a moment, her face bright in the headlights. If I had to choose one word to describe her, it would be trouble – but the exciting kind. The kind you would open the door to, invite right in.

'Who's that?' Jake whispers, and I shake my head, as clueless as he is.

The girl pushes open the iron gate and walks towards the house, and I wonder if she's visiting Louisa Winter, or perhaps if she's here to audition for the band.

I have no way of knowing – and that's OK.

Sometimes the story goes on without you.

I close my eyes and picture a different future, one without a spotlight shining on me. I picture a girl who isn't perfect, a family who don't need her to be, a new baby sister who thinks she's awesome and a boy with tawny-blond hair who likes her just the way she is. There will be meds to take and exams to pass and sometimes bad things will still happen, but I'll cope.

'Cold?' Jake asks. 'C'mon, I'll walk you home.'

I slide down from the wall, brushing leaves the colour of burnished gold from my skirt, and Jake takes my hand in his.

As we walk, the indigo sky explodes suddenly with soft pops and bangs and bright waterfalls of fireworks. Next week it'll be Bonfire Night, and someone in the park must be partying early. I laugh and lean into Jake, the two of us gazing upward, inhaling the heavy smell of smoke and sulphur, watching the cascade of light.

perfectly_imperfect_sometimes

389 likes

perfectly_imperfect_sometimes Ever get fed up with pretending to be something you're not? Me too. Let's get real! Sasha x

Afterword

My daughter had absence seizures for a number of years. I saw first-hand how hard it was to navigate adolescence while battling them, and although Cait eventually grew out of the condition, she asked if I would write about the subject to help other kids feel less alone with it. This book grew from that request, and from talking to other teens and pre-teens coping with absence seizures.

Anxiety is another issue many struggle with, and one that can sabotage things if ignored. Sasha tries to hide her problems, but comes to see that asking for help is the only way forward. If there's something worrying you, I hope you too will be brave enough to ask for help from a parent, teacher, counsellor, doctor or friend.

Take care,

Cathy x

If you need support, information and advice, here are two helpful organizations:
– the Epilepsy Society: www.epilepsysociety.org.uk
– Young Minds: www.youngminds.org.uk (for help with anxiety and other mental health issues)

Read on for an extract from
Sami's Silver Lining

The sun rises slowly over the island in a blur of red and gold – I think it will be the last thing I ever see.

My breathing is raw, ragged, and I'm struggling to keep my head above the crashing waves. I think that I have swallowed half the Aegean Sea, that I might as well stop fighting, give in to it, let myself sink down beneath the surface and die.

I am cold, so cold my limbs feel like ice, and the salt that crusts my lips feels like frost. The island looks closer now, but it might as well be a million miles away because I have no more fight left in me – I have nothing at all. Another

wave lifts me and carries me forward, leaving me face down in the shallows. My hands claw at wet, gritty sand, and I lie exhausted, frozen, gasping for air.

All is lost.

1

Lucky

They say I am lucky, the luckiest boy alive. They say that I must be brave and strong to have survived the hardships life has thrown at me, that I have been given a chance for a new beginning and must grab that chance with both hands.

I am lucky, lucky, lucky . . . or so they tell me.

I didn't choose any of this, and new beginnings feel empty and hollow when you have nobody to share them with.

Well, I have my aunt, my uncle and two grown-up cousins I've barely met. But although they have opened their arms and their hearts to me, I cannot do the same. I cannot let myself care any more, because I am not as strong as people think. I am broken, useless, like a piece of damaged pottery

that looks whole but can never be the same again. I look OK on the outside, but inside I am flawed, fractured.

I am not what people think.

I am a fifteen-year-old boy held together with glue and good luck. There will come a time when my luck runs out, and I will fall apart. The world will see that I was damaged and hurting all along, and perhaps people will understand me a little better. Of course, it will be too late by then.

Sometimes I wish that we had never left Syria, even though our city was a war zone, and everyone an enemy. The government my father and mother once respected had turned against the people, and rebels took to the streets to fight back. Then came the extremists, like vultures feeding on carrion, bringing harsh new laws that dragged us all back to the dark ages. We prayed for the west to help us, but when help arrived it came in the form of western bombs that rained down from the skies and destroyed what was left of the place I once called home.

Sometimes I wish that we had stayed in the refugee camp, even though we were crammed three families to a tent, each tent so close they were almost touching. So close that sickness spread faster than wildfire.

I wish we hadn't taken passage on that boat to Kos, but my father said it would be one step closer to Britain, where my mother's brother lived. Uncle Dara and Aunt Zenna would give us shelter. Sometimes I wish I had stopped fighting then and sunk beneath the waves of the Aegean Sea, the way my father, my mother and my sister did.

I was the lucky one.

I swallowed down my grief, carried it inside me, but it was like a parasite that gnawed away at everything that was good. Eventually I got to the mainland and joined a long line of people who were walking across Europe. I walked until the soles of my boots were worn away, until I had gathered a group of kids around me, who like me were travelling alone. We stuck together because it was safer that way, but still we faced danger every day. We grew tough and cynical and ruthless, and we cried silently at night for all that we had lost. At a camp on the Italian border, charity workers tried to find us places to live. I told them I had family in Britain, and after a long wait they managed to trace my uncle and aunt and get me added to the last consignment of unaccompanied refugee minors to be allowed into the UK.

All I knew of my aunt and uncle were the stories my parents had told and a vague idea that they ran a tailor's shop in London. In fact, they didn't live in London at all, and the tailor's shop was actually a dry-cleaner's, but the charity that was helping me back then tracked them down anyway.

I remember the first time I saw Uncle Dara and Aunt Zenna, standing on the pavement outside the shop to welcome me, the nephew they hadn't even known they had. They were older than my parents, but Dara had a look of my mother all the same: dark wavy hair, stern brows, eyes that glinted with the promise of mischief.

'My little sister Yasmine's boy!' my uncle said, anguished. 'After all this time, how can it be? You are welcome here, Sami. We are family, yes?' He threw his arms around me and I felt the dampness of his tears against my cheek.

I was safe.

I was lucky.

I was home.

My father liked to look at the stars. He would sit on the flat roof of our old house in Damascus, where the railings were lined with terracotta pots of tomatoes, aubergines and peppers, and the warm breeze was heavy with the scent of jasmine, and we'd gaze at the big dark canopy of the night sky.

'Play the flute for us, Sami,' my father would say, and I'd work my way through my scales yet again, squeaky and slow. I got better, of course, until I could play pretty well, until I could provide a soundtrack for my father to look at the stars.

'Head in the clouds,' my mother would say, but there were rarely any clouds back then — just acres of sky, cool as silk, pierced with little bursts of silver light.

My father loved the night sky so much that he moved the old brass bedstead up to the roof. He and my mother slept there, while my little sister Roza and I would lie on our narrow beds in the room below and listen to the whisper of their voices, faint and reassuring, like distant birdsong. If it rained, which was rare, my mother would grab the pillows and the coverlet, and run down into the house, and my father would grab the bedroll and follow her.

Cathy Cassidy

the chocolate box series

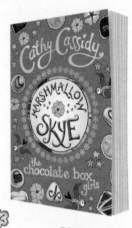

Cherry:
Dark almond eyes, skin the colour of milky coffee, wild imagination, feisty, fun . . .

Skye:
Wavy blonde hair, blue eyes, smiley, individual, kind . . .

Summer:
Slim, graceful, pretty, loves to dance, determined, a girl with big dreams . . .

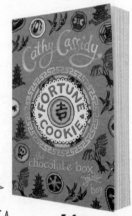

Coco:
Blue eyes, fair hair, freckles, a tomboy who loves animals and wants to change the world . . .

Honey:
Willowy, blonde, beautiful, arty and out of control, a rebel . . .

Jake:
Jake is about to discover that you can't outrun destiny . . .

www.cathycassidy.com

Summer Fruit Skewers

For a refreshing healthy snack on those hot summer days, try making your own garden of fruit skewers.

You will need:

Your fave fruits (the best ones include kiwis, strawberries, grapes, oranges, and watermelon and pineapple slices)

10 or more wooden skewers

Heart, flower or butterfly cookie cutters

A shoe box (this will be your garden display)

What to do:

Using a chopping board carefully cut your chosen fruit into round shapes.

One at a time, lay your slices of fruit on the board and cut into flower, butterfly and heart shapes using the cookie cutters.

Carefully insert the skewers into the fruit to create a beautiful flower display.

Making a Flower:

Cut a slice of pineapple into a flower shape and add to the skewer so it's horizontal. Then add a small strawberry to the very top to make the centre of the flower. Add a couple of grapes to the 'stem' of the flower to look like leaves. Try other methods and designs too!

Assemble Your Flower Garden:

Decorate your shoe box to make it look like a garden, using green paint, tissue paper, flower stickers, etc.

Cut small holes into the top of the shoe box.

Insert your flower skewers into the holes to create a flower border!

Top Tip!
For an extra-refreshing taste, serve with a yoghurt or cream-cheese dip!

www.cathycassidy.com